BENEATH
HIS STARS

The Stars Duet Book 1

Laura,
Don't forget
to look up!
♡ Amie Knight

Amie Knight

Beneath His Stars
Copyright © 2018 Amie Knight

ISBN-13: 978-1727687545
ISBN-10: 172768754X

Editor: Emily Lawrence of Lawrence Editing

Proofreading: Julie Deaton of Deaton Author Services

Interior Design and Formatting: Stacey Blake of Champagne Book Design

DEDICATION

To Jackson and Violet. Never forget, the darkest nights
sometimes produce the brightest stars. So, don't forget
to always look up. Love you to the moon and back.
Better yet, I love you to Pluto and back.

PROLOGUE

Liv

Present

Only in the darkness can you see the stars. I knew that better than anyone. He did, too, only for different reasons.

He lived in the dark.

I worshipped the stars.

What a pair we were.

I'd praised them, basked in their twinkling lights.

He'd hidden among them, covered in the shadows of their night.

I'd danced under their glittering radiance.

He'd concealed himself in the darkness surrounding them.

A sky of dreams. That's what they were to me.

But he was adamant that my dreams were just clouds of helium, hydrogen, and dust that began to collapse under their own gravitational attraction. He'd point to the sky, his face serious, his eyes grave and tell me that as that cloud collapses, the material at the center begins to heat up. Me snuggled between his legs, our behinds to the hard ground, he'd say "A star's born right there at that hot core in the heart of a collapsing cloud, Luna. That cloud had to die for your dreams." He'd sneer.

He says science and I say dreams.

I was silly, then. Just a young girl with too many ideals, too many wishes, and I depended on all of those twinkling lights to make them happen. Oh, how I'd matured the last year.

Then, I thought it so beautiful how much we were like the stars. He and I. Our light and dark. Only, now, I realized how unfortunate it was for us how much we had in common with the stars I loved so. How we united under the most strenuous of circumstances. Carefully, slowly and even though we may have tried to fight it, we couldn't. We were helplessly pulled and twisted together by some unknown, magical force. And we formed. When we finally came together, it wasn't just hot. It was fire. We could have burned the world down. Maybe we did. Maybe we'd burned too bright. Too big. Until we'd just snuffed out.

But how could that be? I still burned for him.

A star was realized.

A dream was born.

But even stars and dreams die.

And God, my heart ached because of it.

Tick. Tick. The clock on the wall read 3:25. Five minutes and I'd be free. Not free to leave. Or free to love. Or really free at all. But free from this classroom and its eyes. I swallowed the lump of emotion in my throat and saliva filled my mouth even as my stomach rolled. I felt sick. But I couldn't think about him here. Not where people could see me. Not where I had to share him.

I stared at the calendar next to the whiteboard as my knee bounced restlessly beneath the desk and my heart raced.

Don't cry, Livvy. His voice slid through my mind so effortlessly, so freely, it could have been my own. My lips trembled even as my pulse slowed. Even though he was miles and miles away, his calm washed over me like a wave rolling up on the beach.

Four days. Four days since I'd been here. My own personal hell. Four long days since I'd seen him. Since I'd smelled him. Since I felt him. Closing my eyes, I took a calming breath. The galaxies behind my eyelids made me snap them back open.

The screech of a chair across the tile floor drew my attention and my gaze inadvertently landed on the girl next to me. Her eyes widened, and I lowered my head as I heard her rushed whisper to the girl next to her. "What the hell is wrong with her?"

There was a hell of a lot wrong with me. Wrong with the world.

The not quite familiar bell rang and still I shot to my feet and practically ran from the classroom and then the building, the sense of suffocation making me fly. My flip-flops slapped against the pavement angrily as I crossed the courtyard to the entrance of the dormitory where I paused and looked up the four floors to my window. I hated that window, this building. I gulped in big breaths, praying for the ability to breathe that never came.

The memory of my stepmother's always contained voice washed over me. "This is for your own good, Livingston. He's just a phase. It'll pass. You'll see." She'd patted me on the head, like an animal, not a daughter. "You'll thank me later," she'd said right here in this very spot. Her pale pink cardigan had blown in the breeze over her perfectly ironed-to-death white blouse.

I'd stared at the pearls around her neck past the point of pissed off and right into enraged territory. "If he's just a phase and it'll pass then why the hell am I here?" I'd gritted from between my teeth.

"You'll watch your mouth, Livingston. Young ladies do not speak that way."

He wasn't just a phase. He wasn't *just* anything. How could he be anything when he was everything?

Even at seventeen, I knew. He was my one—the star that shined brightest in my sky.

I skipped the elevator and the people I knew would occupy it and headed for the stairwell. I couldn't deal with the new-girl stares. Climbing the stairs quickly, I felt them. The tears I worked so hard to keep at bay all day. They hit my eyes like twin pools before trailing down my face and down my neck. There were too many tears to count. Too much sadness to carry. I pressed my hand to my chest hard. I wanted to reach in there and grab my heart, toss it down the stairs. How could it be the source of my life and yet hurt me so badly, too? Instead, I pushed the door open at the top of the stairwell and dashed to my bedroom on the fourth floor. Throwing the door open, a sob hit my throat. I couldn't hold it in any longer. It echoed throughout the room and only made the ache in my chest worse. Relieved and equal parts devastated I was alone, I fell onto my bed face first, clutching my pillow to my face. My tears quickly soaked the fabric and my pillow barely muffled my cries.

This was it. I was going to die of heartbreak. That's what this was, right? I'd never experienced something so debilitating. So excruciating. So awful. I hadn't felt this way since I'd lost my father.

How would I go on without him? Would he forget me? About us? About the stars? Where was he now? Was he okay? Was he as torn up as I was? I rolled to my side and pulled my legs to my chest and held them there, rocking my body.

And I did what I'd done for the past days I'd been here. I thought of him. Of his clear blue eyes framed by the thickest, darkest lashes I'd ever seen. I thought of the tiny crinkles around those eyes when he bestowed one of his rare smiles on me. Those smiles that made me feel like the only girl in the world. I pictured his wide, pink lips when he smiled, that one crooked tooth in the front of his mouth that stole my damn heart over a year ago.

I went back to Adam Nova and his bad boy attitude. His one-word answers that drove me crazy. His too-long dark hair I loved to run my hands through. His way of loving me that compared to no other.

I went back to our space and time. To the field that separated our lives as much as it did our hearts.

To the beginning. To the beginning of the end.

I lay there in that dorm room remembering us. Remembering when I lay beneath our stars. When I lived beneath *his* stars.

CHAPTER 1

Liv

Past

"**W**ait up, Liv!" I heard from behind me, but I pretended I didn't. I was on a mission and that mission was to get as far away from this school as I could get in the smallest amount of time.

"Liv! I know you hear me."

Oh, for heaven's sake, but he wasn't giving up. I rolled my eyes. Braden was dumb, but he wasn't that dumb, apparently. Who would have thought?

I plastered a contrived smile onto my face and pivoted on a heel. Sticking my thumbs inside the bookbag straps that sat on my shoulders, I asked, "What's up?"

I didn't give a diddly what was up, really. I just wanted to get him off my back and get to where I was going. After a full day of playing pretend with my pretentious schoolmates and an hour more of piano lessons I only endured for my stepmother's sake, I just wanted out of there. I wanted to get home, wolf down my dinner as fast as I possibly could, and hide in my room. And then the stars.

I quirked an eyebrow at Braden that could only be described as get the hell on with it.

He danced back and forth on his feet nervously and ran a hand through his blond hair, but I knew better. His horse and pony show weren't fooling me. However, his next words did shock me. "Are you going to homecoming?"

Was he asking me out? Oh, God, no. This was not happening. He had to be kidding me. I felt my brown eyes widen in panic as I looked around the courtyard for any noticeable signs of escape. I wasn't going to the homecoming dance. I especially wasn't going with Braden. Why the hell was he asking me? I stared down at my white Keds that fed into what we in the South liked to call the boniest legs ever and then up at my schoolgirl uniform complete with navy blue pleated skirt and white polo. Yes, I realized, I was a walking cliché. I even annoyed myself.

There were plenty of girls floating around who didn't have bony legs. That weren't too tall. All I had going for me in the boy department were my too big breasts, and well, they were too big. He could have had any girl at Saint Ashley Preparatory. Which meant he could pretty much have any fancy ass girl on the whole ridiculously posh island of Saint Ashley itself.

After all, Saint Ashley was so small we all knew each other. Too well, if you asked me. Everyone was always in somebody else's business. The island dynamic was all too incestuous for my tastes. Saint Ashley sat right off the coast of Madison, South Carolina. I'd call the island more of a resort than an actual place to live. The natives were ridiculously wealthy, living in monstrosities they called mansions that dotted the east coast of the island and the children were disgustingly spoiled. We had one school, K through twelve. One grocery store. And God only knew how the modest Piggly Wiggly in the middle of town was still around, but there it stood, even if it had a fancy coffee shop inside. That grocery store was really the only thing normal about Saint Ashley and it truly wasn't all that normal. Basically, what I'm getting at is that Livingston Montgomery belonged on this island about as much as a fish belonged on dry land.

I was a fish out of water or at least that was what it felt like most days. Don't get me wrong. I was rich. Loaded if you asked my stepmother, but I came from humble beginnings. The people on this island, they were born rich. They'd die rich and they'd never know a day of struggle in their lives. They were what the South liked to call old money. Old money held respect. I was new money, or I'd be new money at the age of twenty-one when I inherited my father's fortune, and no one around here thought new money was worth much at all. And me, I was tired and bored and restless wading through the masses of Louboutin, Versace, and Benzes. These people prided themselves on their belongings, not who they were. Which was exactly why I could never go out with Braden.

3

He was quarterback of our football team, which the whole island fawned over, but the truth was, they sucked. Bad.

Braden had somehow managed to fool the rest of the girls at this school with his demure act, but he didn't fool me. He could fake it with the best of them. Even his wholesome good looks couldn't snare me. Like now, the adorable shy way he bowed his head, his long blond locks covering his eyes, or how he rocked from foot to foot in a show of nervousness, but I knew there wasn't a bashful bone in Braden's body. He came off modest, almost shy. But I'd seen and heard the things he'd done. After all, he was my lovely stepbrother's best friend.

Seeing no way out of the conversation, I turned around and started heading back in the direction I was going. "Not gonna happen, Braden."

I wasn't being mean, but there was no way in hell I was letting Braden take me anywhere. Besides, Sebastian would lose his damn mind. Not that I cared, but I didn't need him breathing down my back anymore than he already did.

"Wait up, Liv." A warm hand landed on my shoulder. I blew out a long, tired breath before turning and facing Braden. I was scrambling and looking for any excuse to say no. He was making me feel trapped and I didn't do trapped.

"Sebastian won't like it," I threw out there like the winning pitch at a baseball game. I was playing dirty, but that was the name of the game in Saint Ashley.

Braden's pretty boy looks fell and I almost felt bad

until I remembered how I'd heard him and my step-brother talk about girls. How they demeaned and disrespected every girl they dated. He brought his hand to run through his hair and gave a good show of flexing his big biceps. I felt like my eyes were going to roll out of my head and my guilt flew out the window right along with my patience.

"Can I go now?" My shoulder brushed his as I started a speedy twelve-minute walk home.

He stepped in beside me. "Seb won't care." His voice was gruff, determined, and I realized this was going to be harder than I thought. He really did want to take me out. It was comical. We'd known each other for years, and he'd never put the moves on me. What had changed?

A bitter laugh flew from my lips. "Sebastian will kill you dead, Braden, and you know it. Why do you want to go out with me, anyway? The bimbo brigade finally catch on to your ways?"

He had every girl in the school falling at his feet. Drooling for his boyish good looks and sweet ride.

Reaching up, he grabbed a thick strand of long brown hair between his fingers and rubbed. I pulled my head back and picked up speed.

"I've always liked you, Liv."

I shook my head and felt my face get red in embarrassment. "No, you haven't."

He stopped on the sidewalk suddenly enough to make me stop, too, and our bodies brushed. I flinched at the contact.

"I don't give a shit what Sebastian says anymore. I want you."

The look in his eyes reminded me all too much of Sebastian's and I felt my skin crawl, but I was no shrinking violet. I'd learned at the tender age of ten when my dad had married the she-devil and moved us to this godforsaken place that I would have to be tough. Be strong. Or this island and its people would pull me down and eventually I'd be too far underwater to make it to the surface. It was a good thing I was an incredible swimmer. My daddy had made sure of that before he left me.

"I'm not interested." I pulled my bookbag higher on my shoulders and took off at a jog now, leaving Braden in the dust, his blond hair and good looks just a dot in the distance when I chanced a look back.

I walked the main strip, the sea at my side and a row of beautiful homes at the other. You'd think as a sixteen-year-old girl, I'd be living the dream. Instead, my life felt like some kind of nightmare I couldn't wake up from as I walked the stretch of island feeling like a bowling ball sat in the bottom of my stomach. Going from that school to my home was trading one evil for another. I loathed them both, but I was sixteen. I could endure. I could make it to my twenty-first birthday. Until I inherited the money my dad left me. Until I could get the hell out of here. Until then, I had the stars and my field.

I paused outside of the huge pink stucco home in front of me. I'd been here six years, and still it didn't feel like home and now that my daddy was gone, I knew it never would. After all, it wasn't somewhere he would have picked to live anyway. No, this home, it was all Georgina. Down to the floral rugs and pink towels that hung in the bathroom. It was nauseatingly girlie with a huge side of gaudy. The huge fountain in the middle of our circular drive said it all. Stone mermaids and cupids and hearts and water. It was ridiculous.

My eyes darted to the left and my lip curled at the red convertible BMW in the driveway. Great, Sebastian was home already. Usually, he was at football practice or out gallivanting with his friends or better yet, taking some unsuspecting girl's virginity and then dumping her the next day, which offered me some reprieve from his creepiness. Not today, though.

If it wasn't for my golden retriever, Harry, I probably would have just turned around and headed to the beach or something. I couldn't leave him to suffer alone.

My shoulders slumped as I walked up the front steps and let myself into the huge marble foyer. I shut the front door quietly, but footsteps echoed from the staircase and I knew I wouldn't manage to get to my room unnoticed.

Sebastian. He might have been good-looking to some. In fact, I knew he was if all of the girls mooning over him at school were any indication. But not to me. All I saw was ugly. That ugly was big and dark and it had lived deep inside Sebastian since the very moment I'd met him years ago. It poured out of his ears and eyes like a heavy fog rolling off the ocean in the morning.

Ugly. It was all I saw.

"Livingston." The way he said my name made my mouth fill with saliva. He said it with reverence and filth. His voice was deep and dark with want and deceit. It made me shiver.

He leaned against the wall in the grand stairwell, all fake nonchalance, effectively blocking me from going to my room. Yes, I knew to some Sebastian was beautiful. But I'd seen first-hand what shadows lurked in the depths of this dark boy's soul. His soft, long, brown curls and sparkling white smile didn't deceive me. His playful brown eyes didn't fool me. I knew what kind of games he wanted to play. The disturbing kind.

"Where's Georgina?" I stupidly asked, like she was going to save me. Help me. It was laughable. That woman only thought of one person. Herself.

A bitter laugh passed his lips. "Who the hell knows." He lifted a glass to his lips, taking a sip and finally stepping down the stairs toward me like he owned the place. And in a lot of ways he did. "Who cares."

I didn't move. I didn't back down. I knew from experience the moment I showed weakness he'd be on me like white on rice. It was the fear. He loved it. The predator in him could smell it. He'd roll around in it, wallow in it, and come out the other end smiling like a maniac.

His fancy loafer tapped against the marble floor in front of me and I stood there still as a statue. He was only a year older than me, but it felt like he was miles taller, infinitely stronger.

He leaned in, his nose almost in the crook of my

neck, and I smelled the expensive brandy Georgina liked to keep in the house on his breath. Bile rose in my throat.

He breathed deeply like a man starved for air. He was starved for something and it frightened me. It had since the very beginning. I'd always known.

"Mmmm," he hummed near the skin of my neck and I froze as his nose made its way to my ear, careful to never touch me. No, Sebastian was as smart as he was creepy. He never touched me. He made sure to never do anything that could come back to bite him in the ass later on. He was sadistically patient. He was waiting on the right time to strike. And he'd been doing it for years, keeping me on my toes, always fearful, always dreading.

Panicked but trying to hide it as best as I could, I pushed past him, careful to touch him as little as possible, and darted up the stairs to the sanctuary of my room and the safety it still provided for now. He never came there. It was the only space in the house that was mine.

"You smell good, Livingston. Just how I like you." His deep voice made me pause on the steps. It slid over me like a thousand dirty hands. I felt sick. He always called me Livingston. Him and the evil stepmonster.

I felt the right side of my lips curl up in a smile even as I kept my back to him. I straightened my spine and cleared my throat and prepared to hit him where I knew it would hurt. The sick bastard. I would win today.

"Braden asked me out today." And I ran up the stairs like a bat out of hell, shooed Harry into my room, and slammed the door behind us as I heard a glass shatter downstairs.

Yes, my stepbrother, Sebastian Carter West, was good at playing sick games, but Livingston Rose Montgomery was getting better and better at it, too, and it frightened the hell out of me.

CHAPTER 2

Liv

I was thirteen the first time I crossed the bridge on foot from Saint Ashley Island to the mainland. Tonight, I was alone, but back then I hadn't been. Tonight, I was like a thief, stealing off into the night, but the only thing I took with me were my memories.

My daddy's strong hand had enveloped mine as we walked across all those years ago. The smell of old spice in my nose, the tanginess of salt on my lips, the rare car meandering past. It had been a slow walk, almost a stroll. By then, he'd been barely able to walk, but he'd made it across that bridge somehow. He didn't say much. He didn't have to. We were as close as two people could be, me and him.

We often communicated through small smiles, little looks we threw each other. Yeah, we knew each other in and out. Words weren't too much needed with us. And there were little that night as we walked along the sidewalk on the bridge that separated the mainland from the island. My hand was warm in my daddy's. I'd never forget it. It would forever be one of those nights that was burned into my mind. Mostly because it was the night my daddy told me he'd be leaving me soon. A part of me had already known, but a bigger part of me had been in denial. He was all I had left. My mother had died giving birth to me. Surely, fate wouldn't take my daddy, too.

We'd finished crossing the bridge and entered a huge field to the right side of the road. We'd walked deep into the grassy field until all you could see was the bridge in the distance and the stars in the sky, the ocean far off, but not so far you couldn't hear its waves. He'd pulled out a blue blanket he'd had tucked underneath his left arm and laid it in the grass.

Tonight, I laid that same blue blanket down, only instead of lying down next to my daddy with my hand in his, I lay down alone, much like I did most nights I could sneak out here. And I did what he told me to do.

"Look at the stars, Liv. If you feel alone. If you feel sad. I'll always be there." He'd leaned over me, his solemn green eyes pinning me to the ground, holding me together. He laid his hand on my chest. "And here." He'd thrummed his fingers against my heart and I thought at that moment that maybe my heart would just stop. I had wanted it to. I'd wanted to go with him. I'd even prayed for it in the months that followed.

"Don't forget to look up, Liv."

Wetness had filled my eyes and run down the sides of my almost-a-woman cheeks. *It's not fair*, I'd wanted to yell. *How can I lose both my momma and you*, I'd wanted to scream. But I hadn't. For him. I only gave him a sad smile as tears pooled in my small ears and the temples of my brown hair. He'd blown out a relieved breath and lain back against the blanket, clutching my hand in his own and bringing it to rest over his heart. I'd felt it beat against the back of my hand. I breathed in the ocean air and the smell of my daddy in that field underneath the stars. It would be the last time we were alone. The last time we could just be. Before the rush of visitors. The wave of goodbyes. Before the morphine and prayers and endless parade of people and hospice nurses.

Look at the stars, Liv. If you feel alone. Don't forget to look up. I was always alone. A stranger in my own skin. Just a girl with a bucket full of dreams and a past full of ghosts. But still, I looked at the stars and I wished. I dared to dream. For my daddy, a dreamer himself. For a man who'd built his life from the ground up. For my momma, for a better life. For love. And I talked to my mother and father as they hid among the stars. I told them of my day, and I prayed they heard. I wished on a shooting star. I prayed for peace. Not for the world, because even at sixteen, I was still wholly selfish. No, I prayed for peace within myself. And strength to go on when it felt like I had no one on my side.

I didn't know it then, but that would be the last time my daddy crossed that bridge by car or foot until the day he died.

I knew it, now. God, I knew it and I hated it.

So, I came here at night when life became too hard.

To my field of dreams and my sky of wishes. I tried not to cry tonight. It hadn't been so bad. Sebastian had only been his usual self. But it hadn't been him I was disappointed in. It was myself. It was like I was turning into these people. Becoming malicious and mean. Thoughtless and selfish; vengeful. A calmness only this field could give me settled over me. I felt my daddy here. I could almost imagine him lying next to me.

I rolled on the blanket until I was on my side, facing away from the island and toward the lights of Madison. My daddy said it wasn't safe for me there. But it wasn't safe for me here, either. Madison was beautiful with its old Southern charm, antebellum homes, and Spanish moss. But not this side. This was the north side and it kept me chained to this island and this field like a prisoner to jail. I was too scared. I wasn't brave or heroic. I'd been sheltered from that bad. Maybe because my life had already suffered too much bad. I was still a kid with a healthy dose of fear her father had instilled in her as soon as he'd brought me there.

Still, I'd adventured over that way some and I knew if I crept closer to the north side of that field, cigarettes, broken bottles, and old condom wrappers littered it. I'd always turned around and headed back to my blue blanket and dreams. Because I knew what lay on the other side of that bridge and field in North Madison.

I'd seen it enough on days my daddy had taken me out. We'd crossed the bridge from the safety of our luxury car and I'd pressed my face to the window every time, barely understanding what I was seeing. It was like some weird dream, leaving the beautiful island of Saint Ashley and two minutes later entering what could only be described as the ghetto where homelessness, prostitution, and drugs were rampant. The demographic divides in Madison were staggering, even to my young eyes. Even I knew it was wrong. It was like Madison had two classes. The really rich and the really poor.

I told myself, I'd get out one day and I'd make a difference. I could do a lot with the money my father left me. I wouldn't sit on that island for the rest of my life and live blissfully unaware of what was going on around the world. I could change things. I could help.

Days like today made me think I couldn't, but I knew different. I felt stuck today. The confrontation with Sebastian sat heavily on me. I was tired of it. Just done. I turned back to the sky and crossed my legs at the ankle and closed my eyes. It was weird. How I felt safer in this open field under the stars than I did at my home.

A rustle of grass and the snap of what sounded like a twig drew my attention and I sat up quickly, looking around. Most nights I brought my big goofy golden retriever for the little protection he offered me. He was sweet and wouldn't hurt a fly, but at least he looked somewhat intimidating. But tonight, I'd been very cautious not to wake Sebastian, so I'd left him at home.

I was usually vigilant. I knew from experience I wasn't the only one who came out here, but I knew the bridge side of the field was safer. Clearly, tonight I hadn't been as safe. I hadn't been as watchful. Because three men who looked to be a couple of years older than me surrounded my blue blanket and blacked out my stars with their height. Every hair on my body stood on end as panic filled my chest.

"Damn, boys, look what we have here," the tall one with dark hair said as he stood in front of me. His dirty jeans and faded black T-shirt told me which side of the bridge he was from and I felt a healthy dose of fear.

I had good enough sense to scramble back on the blanket and try to stand, but the ringleader who'd spoken before was lightning fast and dropped into a squat beside me. I pulled at the hem of the white summer dress at my ankles, making sure every inch of me was covered.

He placed a firm hand on my shoulder. "Nah, baby. You're good. You don't need to get up on our account." His greasy brown eyes moved from my face and down over my body. His hand moved from my shoulder to my ankle and my whole body stiffened at the contact, but I tried my best to put on a brave front.

"Come on, man. Leave her alone." My eyes left my ankle and darted to the man behind greasy guy. The tall blond behind him ran a hand through his hair. "Let's go." He looked at the man standing beside him for help and my eyes shot to his, too, hoping for something. Only there didn't seem like there'd be any help there.

The guy was staring at me. Not in the way Sebastian did, but in a way like he was trying to figure me out. Like he was studying me. I swallowed hard as I took in his icy blue eyes almost hidden behind his long black bangs. But no, it wasn't those eyes that made me pause. That kicked up my pulse. He was covered in tattoos. They didn't just peek out of the sleeves of his shirt. No, this man wore his tattoos like clothes. They blanketed his arms and came out of the top of his shirt and onto his neck. He intimidated me. Maybe it was the tattoos. Maybe it was the chilly blue eyes or maybe it was that he wasn't smiling and didn't look at all like he was going to help me. No, he looked like he wanted to unwrap me and study all my parts. The intensity was blistering, his stare unwavering.

I was fucked. And I didn't use fuck lightly. I'd never actually had someone approach me out here. Had I seen people before who frightened me? Yes. But I'd always left before they'd made contact. I'd always gotten the hell out of there. Never had I been cornered and definitely not by three men, two of which looked like they could eat me alive in one big bite. I swallowed a golf ball size lump of fear.

I weighed my options on that blanket. I'd get up and leave. I'd run. They might catch me, but I was long and fast. Although, the flip-flops on my feet might slow me down. I'd ditch them. I'd run. I'd fight, even if my fear made me stumble.

The guy crouched down next to me smirked. "What are you doing all alone out here, baby?" He looked toward Saint Ashley before darting his eyes back to mine. "You're from the island, right? You out slumming it tonight?" His fingers skirted up my ankle and to the sensitive skin behind my knee. Fear climbed up my throat. I jerked back, frightened and pissed off, my pulse jumping in my throat so hard I could feel it all over me, all inside of me.

"Come on, Boone. Let's get out of here," the blond guy pleaded and pulled on the sleeve of Boone's shirt. All the while, tattoo guy stared at me, his piercing eyes seeming to see right through me to the other side of the field. I couldn't tell if he wanted to kick me or taste me. It was unnerving.

I couldn't believe this. How many times a day could a girl get accosted? I'd come out here for a break. My eyes met the blond's and I mentally pleaded with him. Jesus, even my field under the stars wasn't safe anymore. I felt so helpless. I tried to stand up, but the man they called Boone only brought his hand around my knee and pushed down, keeping me seated. Fear hit my skin like ice and tears invaded my eyes. I was truly screwed. I was going to be raped and possibly killed in my daddy's field. I'd be a statistic. I'd be another stupid girl, who made a dumb decision and became a number.

I met the tattooed guy's blue eyes again and they drifted down to the spot where Boone had his hand on my knee. His eyes focused on Boone's hand and they froze there, chilling me to the bone.

I pressed my eyes closed, praying for someone, something, anything really.

"That's enough."

My lids shot open and my eyes once again hit blue orbs.

I noticed all eyes were on him now. It was stated

so plainly, so unexpectedly, so brutally, that we all just watched and waited.

"Now," he finished succinctly, his pink lips curling around the word slowly, adamantly. It was a command. An order. Definitely not a request. His firm voice like a thunderclap in the middle of the quiet field, his face unreadable.

Boone rolled his eyes and blew out a breath, his hand dropping from my leg. "Fine. Let's go. She's probably a fucking virgin, anyway." He stood up quickly and brushed off his pants, like he hadn't just scared the shit out of me and acted like an animal. I looked at the man with the tattoos, my eyes trying to tell him how thankful I was, but he only stared at me. His blue eyes bored. His face blank.

He turned and headed back to the north side of Madison, not even sparing me another glance, the blond scampering behind him, throwing apologetic looks over his shoulder.

It was Boone who left last with the parting words, his slippery gaze sliding over my body once more. "Better be careful out here by yourself at night, baby. It's dangerous, ya know?"

It was a threat, but it felt like a promise. I did know. And now I knew even more. Nowhere was safe.

CHAPTER 3

Adam

The sting of the needle felt good. Too good. I shivered as Raven pressed the ink into my skin at the base of my neck. I was particularly sensitive there. Some might believe that's why I came here. Because I liked the pain. Because maybe I got off on it, but that wasn't the truth. The truth was my tattoos were the perfect disguise. I hid behind the pieces of art that covered my body. Every color, every picture was a story that hid mine. And I liked it like that. When people looked at me, they didn't see me. They saw my ink. They didn't want to talk to me. They didn't want to know me. I loved it. I hated it.

"Almost done here." Raven smiled down at me from behind her pierced nose and shaggy black hair. We'd been friends since grade school and she'd been practicing her craft on me for as long as I could remember. I'd been the perfect blank canvas in high school and now at the age of nineteen my torso and arms and most of my neck were almost completely covered. Hidden. Just how I liked it.

"Take your time." I didn't have anywhere to be. It was one of my rare days off from work. Another place I could hide. And I didn't feel like roaming the streets with Boone and Grady, getting into God knows fucking what with them. There wasn't really much else do to on this side of Madison, South Carolina. I was nineteen, poor as sin like the rest of this side of the city. Barely scraping by on the minimal wages of my part-time job and trying my damnedest to put myself through school at the local technical college. The only thing I had going for me was Raven and the free tattoos she gave me.

Raven was my saving grace in a lot of ways. We'd been together since elementary school. She'd sat next to me in kindergarten and that had been all she wrote. We were two socially awkward kids who bonded over our awkwardness. We'd never dated. It was always out of the question, mostly because Raven was a lesbian and I was, well, an asshole. She knew all my secrets. All of my fears and insecurities. And while she looked like a total badass with her black hair, nose piercing, and abundance of tattoos, she was still the kindest, most understanding person in my life.

"Not working today?" she asked over the buzz of the tattoo gun, her eyes never leaving the tattoo needle.

"Nah."

Her right eyebrow lifted. "Not hanging with your boys." Her voice smacked of snark and I felt myself almost smile. Raven didn't care much for Boone and

Grady. Not that I blamed her. Over the years they had proven they were definitely more trouble than they were worth. Boone seemed to be taking the assholery up a notch lately.

"Nah." I didn't have the stomach for him tonight. Like Raven, I'd known him and Grady since we were kids. We weren't as close as Raven and I were, but we'd lived in the same busted ass apartment building our entire lives. It seemed like the older we got, the crazier Boone was getting. Part of me understood. He felt stuck, like the rest of us. Only the older Boone got and the longer he had to endure our circumstances, the less fucks he had. He was getting downright scary. And annoying as fuck.

Amid the buzz and burn of the needle I thought of the girl in the park. The one in the white dress and dark hair from two nights before. The one Boone had put his hands on. I felt my fist clench and heard the crack of my knuckles. It had made me irrationally angry. I was quiet and reserved and usually I let Boone carry on. What did I give a fuck if he touched one of the rich bitches from the island? I knew he wouldn't actually hurt her. Scare the shit out of her maybe, but that wasn't my problem. Or it had never been my problem before. But the fear on her face that night had made me pause. In truth, a lot about her made me stop in my tracks. Her looks were unusual. Her legs too skinny, her face too long. The juxtaposition of her wide mouth and small upturned nose was startling, but what really made me pause were her eyes. They were dark, chocolate brown with the thickest, richest eyelashes I'd ever seen.

And despite my desire to walk away and let Boone have his fun I hadn't been able to ignore those eyes. They'd screamed for help, those sad, dark orbs. Stupid girl. She shouldn't have been out there. It was dangerous. Too many kids from the island didn't understand the same rules didn't apply to the north side of Madison that it did to their precious island. It was a dog eat dog world over here. We worked, we stole, we hustled. We didn't have the luxury of gazing at the fucking stars for fun.

Still, my mind couldn't help but wander back to her from time to time and it pissed me off. How had a girl lying in a field under the stars made me so irrationally angry? It was because I worried for her. And I didn't need another fucking worry in my life. I had enough on my plate caring and taking care of my crippled father. Only, I couldn't help it. I couldn't help but think that she wouldn't be so lucky the next time she crossed that bridge. How many times had she already pushed her luck? Fuck, but for all I knew she could be out there now. Her white dress fanned around her. From a distance she'd looked like the moon against the backdrop of the millions of stars in the sky above her. But she'd definitely looked like she'd lain there before. She'd been too comfortable on that soft looking pale blue blanket underneath her, and I couldn't help but hope and pray she'd learned a lesson that night and stayed the hell out of that field and on her safe island that may as well have been a completely different world.

"How's my *papi chulo*?" Raven's voice disrupted my thoughts.

I rolled my eyes. "For fuck's sake. Stop calling my dad that shit. It's gross."

She shrugged. "What? Even as a lesbian, I can appreciate a sexy Hispanic man." Her dark eyebrows waggled.

My Puerto Rican father had that effect on people. I guess most women did think he was handsome. Even with his bum leg, he could still pull the ladies and he did so often. He was brutally robbed five years ago walking home from his job as a mechanic downtown. He'd recovered mostly. Well, except for his right leg, which would forever be fucked. He couldn't get up and down off the floor like he used to. Working on cars really wasn't an option and disability only paid so much and that was why I'd had a job since I was fifteen years old. It was also why I felt like I could never leave this shitty town and my even shittier circumstances.

I studied Raven's face. My father adored her. And she adored him. They had a healthy, disturbingly hilarious father daughter relationship since Raven's own father had long since dipped out on her and her mother. I wondered if maybe that was why Raven didn't like most men. Me and papa were it for her.

"He's good. He asked me this morning when you were coming by. Says you haven't been to see him lately."

She arched an eyebrow at me. "I haven't been invited."

Shaking my head, I threw back, "You know you don't have to be invited, asshole."

She pursed her lips and smiled. "I'm feeling the love, Nova." She gave me a wink.

Raven was a shameless flirt. Even with the sex she had no interest in. Her latest girl was young.

"Speaking of babies. What's going on with you and Aspen?" Raven's newest girl was only seventeen and I was giving her plenty of shit for it. Because that's what we did.

Her eyes rolled back in her head dramatically. "Come on, Nova. She was so last week." She pointed a gloved finger at me. "Besides, she wasn't that young. Only two years younger than us."

She turned the tattoo gun off and dabbed my skin with a paper towel.

"What happened?"

She shrugged. "You know. The usual." She wouldn't meet my eyes. "I'm basically just a fun ride, until they go back to their boyfriends."

Her lips curled in distaste.

A lot of girls liked to experiment with Raven, but weren't really in it for the long haul. It sucked for her, but we were still young, and I knew she would find her person one day.

I sat up, grabbing her arm, and she looked at me and I threw her a smirk. "Don't worry. You'll find someone who's willing to put up with your shit one day."

Now me, that was a completely different story. I doubted I had a person and if I did there was probably a less than 1 percent chance that I would ever meet her. Staying at home, going to school, and working were pretty much my life. It was rare that I had a day to just chill and I wasn't the best at socializing anyway. As Raven liked to tell me, I was a social pariah, even if she did tell me that in a loving kind of way.

I was aloof. I was intimidating. I liked it like that.

And clearly, I wasn't the best at giving pep talks either. Raven pulled her arm away from me and started cleaning up, completely ignoring me poking fun at her.

"You will. You'll meet a nice chick one day, Rav. And ditch my sorry ass." I nudged her with my arm so she would look at me.

And when she did, I tried not to divert my eyes. I didn't like making eye contact. I found the whole ordeal extremely hard.

"How will I meet anybody if I keep hanging out with your scary non-smiling ass?" She turned away, hiding her grin from me.

"You're right. I'm a terrible wingman. But it could be worse. You could be stuck with Boone."

Her lips curled. "Ugh. You know better, Adam. That douche makes my skin crawl."

She was right. Boone was a douche. Hanging out with him was more of a habit than an actual want. I wondered if Boone made the girl in the field's skin crawl. My jaw clenched at the thought. I didn't like that I hated the thought of him making her feel that way.

It was late. Maybe I'd stop by on the way home and check the field. Make sure she wasn't lying out there like a sitting duck again. Maybe I'd make sure she was safe from Boone and anyone else who might happen upon her.

No.

Fuck no.

No. I wouldn't do that. She wasn't mine to take care of.

"What are you thinking about so hard over there?" Raven was rubbing ointment on my tattoo, her eyes darting to mine occasionally.

"What makes you think I'm thinking about anything?"

Pushing out her lips, she answered, "Mostly because you're always thinking about something." She pointed to the middle of my forehead. "And you always get a line there when you're stressing."

I lifted my hand and rubbed the middle of my head, right where she pointed and felt the damn wrinkle, but still I argued, "Not true. And I don't stress."

"True and whatever. I've had to look at your ugly mug my entire life. I know your face better than you do."

I ran my hand down the side of my face. "Some ladies think this mug is pretty hot, Rav."

"Pfttt, they'd feel differently if they knew you like I did." She laughed.

But it almost wasn't funny. She was right. Most women didn't gravitate toward me. Yeah, some girls liked the bad boy persona and the tattoos, but that wore off quickly once they realized I wasn't boyfriend material. That I didn't have time for their games and drama.

Raven finished wrapping me up and I tried to pay her, but as usual she refused. "You're my guinea pig and don't you forget it. I'll probably jack you up one day and that will be payment enough."

I nodded and stretched my fist out, which she quickly bumped. "Come by and see me and Dad this weekend. I'm off Sunday."

"Sure thing."

And I was in the wind. Only tonight there wasn't much wind, even for being this close to the beach. I paused on the sidewalk long enough to light my cigarette. It was September and still hot as hell. Much like it was every year in the Carolinas. We might get some reprieve toward the middle of October.

Somehow, I managed to not walk past the field on the way home. I jumped a couple of fences and cut across yards to avoid it, determined not to check up on the girl who looked like the moon, all bathed in white.

I walked the road with run-down apartment building after run-down apartment building to finally come to mine. Maybe it was good that the girls didn't hang around long. It wasn't like I could bring them back here. Trash, cigarette butts, and a few beer bottles littered the porch. I kicked past them as I entered, almost running smack into Mona.

She gave me a coy smile and I felt that wrinkle in my forehead pop out, this time in frustration. Fuck. Raven was right.

Mona's stoned eyes appraised me while I tried to push past her and climb the seven floors to my apartment. The elevator was slow as hell and I needed to escape.

"Where you off to so fast, baby? You could come inside for a bit." Her voice floated up to me from where I was almost two stories up now. You did not go into Mona's apartment. If you did, you got laid. And then unbeknownst to you, she got paid. And if she didn't she'd show her ass until her drug dealer pimp hunted you down and kicked your ass and then she still got paid. Boone had learned that the hard way. I smiled thinking about it.

I opened the apartment door and found the whole place dead silent. Usually Pops had the TV on and was relaxing in his old beat-up recliner in the front room. I checked the bad eighties style kitchen and found a note on the counter that he went to his friend's Julius's downstairs to play checkers.

I grabbed a soda out of the fridge and paced the apartment feeling restless as I looked out the windows at how dark it was. I treaded across the worn carpet again and again. Our place was clean compared to most others. Just because my dad couldn't work as a mechanic anymore didn't mean he didn't clean and take care of the place. We'd never lived like most of the other people in our building. We took care of our meager belongings. After all, they were all we had.

I sat on the couch and checked my cell phone twice, not really expecting to have any missed calls. There were really only two people who called me and one of them was downstairs and the other I'd just left at work.

Walking to the kitchen to throw away my soda can, I looked outside again, deciding I needed another cigarette. I grabbed my cell phone, my keys, and smokes and headed downstairs. I smoked two cigarettes in front of my apartment building before I couldn't stand it any longer and suddenly I was moving and not in the direction I wanted to. It was like my feet had a mind of their own. I was like a moth to a flame when it came to that girl. I walked the three blocks to the field, feeling like I wasn't me. Like maybe I was someone else. Like maybe I was a crazy person.

It wasn't long before I saw her in the distance, only this time she had a dog lying next to her. I stopped far enough away that she didn't see me but I could still see her.

It was hard to miss her lying on that big blue blanket with the big canine beside her. Why the hell had she come out here again? What was she thinking? It had only been a couple of days since Boone had harassed her. Did she have no sense of self-preservation at all?

A good part of me wanted to march over there and yank her up by her long brown hair and demand she go back to the island. But there was a small part of me that just wanted to watch her.

I realized how weird that was. Still, I felt myself crouch down where the grass was longer and harder to walk through and I watched her talk to herself. I watched her count the stars. I watched her close her eyes for minutes on end, seemingly asleep, but I knew she wasn't because she was obviously one of those restless people who rocked their ankles back and forth when they were trying to be still.

I tilted my head and squinted, trying to catch more than just a blurry off in the distance version of her. Fuck, but I wanted to see more.

I watched her far longer than I should have. I watched her until she finally stood up and grabbed her blanket and snapped it in the air, shaking the grass off. And I watched her fold it and tuck it under her right arm and turn and start walking to the bridge. And then I watched her cross that bridge until I couldn't see her at all anymore.

I should have been concerned about my behavior. I really should have. But all I could think as she faded off into the distance was that next time, I'd bring my binoculars so I could really see her face, so I could see the expression in her eyes.

CHAPTER 4

Liv

"Elbows, Melody Ann!" Ms. Donnelly said from her place at the head of the table.

Mel looked over at me, rolled her eyes, and slowly slid her elbows off the mahogany table beneath them. I brought the napkin from my lap to my face to hide my giggle.

"Please, Ms. Montgomery, sit up. Your posture is that of a ninety-year-old woman. It's positively atrocious."

I wanted to laugh again, but instead I bit my lip. I couldn't agree more. My posture was shit. I was tall and gangly and tried my best to hide my big breasts by stooping over a bit, but my posture didn't have a thing on Ms. Donnelly's house because nothing and I mean nothing was as atrocious as Ms. Donnelly's home.

The place was covered in doilies and porcelain dolls that were propped up in cabinets in the corners and the whole thing just gave me the straight creeps.

Even though I hated how my breasts stuck out when

I sat up, I placed the napkin in my lap and snapped my back straight until it lined up with the back of the hard wooden chair I sat in. I kept my chin parallel to the table and a placid look on my face, taking in the other four girls at the table, all looking as miserable as me. Which was a travesty, if you asked me. We were surrounded by cakes and cookies and tea and this should have been fun, but it was the farthest thing from it.

It was etiquette classes and there wasn't a damn thing fun about them.

"What do you say, Livingston?" Ms. Donnelly sang out too sweetly from the other end of the table, her saccharine smile disturbingly sweet.

"Thank you, Ms. Donnelly." I gave her the biggest and fakest smile I could before averting my eyes to Mel and giving her big eyes. Eyes that said help me before one of her dolls eats me.

She bit her lip and lifted her teacup. At least Mel and I were in this hell together. And hell it was. And even though Mel had been raised with a silver spoon in her mouth, she found this whole thing just as ridiculous as I did. Etiquette classes, dance classes, it was all the loveliness that came with being a Southern debutante. It was all crazy and over the top and if my daddy had been alive, I knew there was no way in hell he'd subject me to this. But I didn't have any other family. Sebastian and Georgina were it. I'd been excited years ago when my daddy had moved us here from only a few hours away in Georgia.

I'd argued with Georgina plenty about it, but she'd

insisted since I was sixteen it was time.

"We Southerners love to celebrate our women, not simply for their beauty and grace, but more importantly for their smarts, wit, and strength. That is what being a deb is about, Livingston," she'd preached at me. That little speech had convinced me to give the whole thing a go. Well, that and I didn't want to hear Georgina's screeching about the whole thing. But I was quickly learning this was more about a bunch of rich upper-class snobs showing off their daughters and how perfect they were and less about my wit and smarts. And charm? Well, everyone knew that wasn't my forte. And these classes were miserable.

"Okay, ladies. You're dismissed, and I expect that you will not be late next Tuesday." Ms. Donnelly shot me and Mel a look that said she meant business and I held back my smirk. I was hoping Ms. Donnelly was learning she shouldn't expect much out of me and Mel at all.

We all pushed our seats back politely and said a very smiley Stepford wife goodbye to Ms. Donnelly and rushed to our backpacks and out the door of her house. *Goodbye potpourri smell!*

"You headed home?" Mel shouted out from behind me in the driveway.

I shrugged. "I've got nowhere else to be."

"You could come and hang out with me, Seb, and Braden?"

My nose scrunched up. Not just no, but hell no I wanted to shout, but instead I shook my head with a sad smile.

Mel and I were friends.

We weren't best friends, but she was one of the few people on the island I trusted and confided in. Mel was good peeps, despite her asshole, uppity family. We'd known each other since I'd moved to the island with my dad. Georgina had introduced us right away, hoping we would be fast friends. Mel's mother was stepmonster's best friend. Their plan had worked in a way. I did like Mel. We'd immediately connected. We just got each other. But I always kept in the back of my mind that she was Sebastian's friend first. They'd known each other their whole lives. She was one of the many, many girls who Seb and Braden had snowballed. Which shocked the hell out of me. Mel was a smart girl. And I couldn't seem to convince her otherwise no matter how I tried.

"I'm gonna pass." I threw my bookbag over my shoulder and walked down the driveway.

Mel caught up with me and nudged her shoulder into mine. "I figured, but you know I had to ask."

I smiled at her, thankful she'd asked even if I'd rather have every one of my fingernails removed with plyers than hang with those assholes.

"What about tomorrow? We don't have piano or etiquette. We could take Harry and Bailey over to the dog park after school?"

I nodded. "Sounds good." And it did. I liked to stay out of the house as much as I could in the evenings. It was getting harder and harder to avoid Sebastian lately. He'd been spending less and less time at football practices and partying with friends and more and more time at home. With me. And I wasn't fool enough to believe he was there for anything but me.

At least tonight I knew he'd be out.

Mel and I parted ways right in front of her house and I walked the rest of the way home, feeling lighter than I had in days, knowing that Sebastian wasn't home.

All that lightness slipped right through my fingers when I saw the black town car in the driveway. Jesus, it was like I couldn't catch a break lately.

Still, I trudged up the steps and into the house ready to face Georgina's wrath. She'd changed since losing my father, or maybe she was just letting her true colors fly since he was gone. I didn't really care why. I just wanted it to stop.

I was lucky today. The house was quiet when I entered except for clicks of Harry's toenails on the tile.

"Hey, buddy. I'm home." I leaned down, giving him a good scrub across the head and he gave me a thank you lick.

I made some dinner as quietly as possible as to not disturb my stepmonster if she did happen to be home and sleeping. After an hour of homework, I leashed Harry up and grabbed my blue blanket. I knew I was a fool, but I couldn't stay away. I didn't know why. I just knew it was where I belonged. And even though I knew it wasn't safe especially after how I'd been cornered a few nights ago, I couldn't seem to keep myself from coming out here. So, we walked down the beach, across the street, and eventually across the bridge. I went to my usual spot in the field, careful to look for anyone. I was laying out my blue blanket when I saw it.

It was one of those old school glass Coke bottles sitting in the grass a couple of feet away. But that wasn't what drew my attention. No, it was the fact it looked to have a piece of white paper inside.

I walked over and picked the bottle up and sure enough, it looked like a note was inside. I smiled, intrigued at the prospect that I might have found someone else's note. Maybe it was a treasure map. Oh! Maybe it was a love letter.

Turning the bottle over, I shook it and shook it to no avail, anxious and excited to see what was written on the paper, if anything was at all. Oh, I hoped there was. This was the most exciting thing that had happened to me in years, it felt like.

Finally, I slid my pointer finger into the top of the bottle alongside the paper and pulled carefully, sure not to tear the paper, and it slipped free. I unfolded it carefully and sure enough there was black writing. My heart kicked up a notch. How freaking exciting.

But then I read the words and I was confused. It wasn't a love note for someone or really even anything that made sense. I plopped down on my blue blanket with the bottle and the paper in my lap, Harry next to me, trying to understand why someone left this in the field and who they'd left it for. It couldn't be me, could it? Did someone else come out here and look at the sky or did someone write this note and stick it in that bottle just for me? I studied it, more confounded than intrigued now.

It's your lucky night tonight. Look up, like you always do. But this time look for a bright, orange star in the sky.

And I did. I looked up, scanning the sky until I saw it. Just like the note said there it sat, the almost red star among the white of the others. I looked down at the note, my heart having left my chest to beat right in the center of my throat. Harry whimpered like he was anxious, too, and laid his head in my lap. I petted him with a shaking hand.

That's Mars, the "red planet." It's closer to the Earth than it has been in fifteen years and it won't be this close again for another seventeen, so lie back and enjoy it while you can.

I flipped the paper over. That was it? I jerked my head up, scanning the field, but not able to see much in the dark. "Helloooo. Hello!" I called out, desperate for someone else to step forward and say this was left for them.

Finally, I stood, Harry joining me. I walked around the blue blanket, looking around carefully. Surely, I was mistaken. Maybe that letter in the bottle was for someone else and not me. That's what I told myself because it scared the hell out of me. But I wasn't a fool. I knew. I was the only one who came to this spot. I was the only one who came here in the night and stargazed. No, it was meant for me and it terrified me. It excited me.

I sat on the blanket, feeling nervous and elated all at

once. I looked around again, thinking of the night the men had surrounded me. Boone had. But maybe the blond who had protected me? Maybe he had come back for me?

I felt an electric buzz underneath my skin. A spark of something new and fresh and exciting.

That had to be it. The blond. Still, I couldn't stay here and wait. That would be stupid. And I wasn't stupid. What I was, was pretty damn scared. So I left, the bottle still in the field, but the note clutched firmly in my hand.

CHAPTER 5

Liv

I was an idiot. Freaking dumb. Silly. A young, foolish, stupid girl who couldn't stop thinking about the bottle and its letter. Not even if I tried. And I did. I really did.

"What's that you got there?" Mel nodded to the piece of paper in my hand.

Busted. Totally busted. But it wasn't the first time in the three days since I'd found the note that I'd studied it. I'd done more than study it, really. I'd obsessed over it. Looking for any clue as to who could have possibly left it. I'd scrutinized the hardly legible letters written haphazardly on a ripped piece of white notebook paper, deciding it had to be a boy or a man. Only a male would write with such carelessness, I'd decided. And I'd flipped the paper over a thousand times it felt like. In the quiet of my room. In the classrooms at school. When I should have been paying attention at etiquette classes and like right now when we were just getting ready to start with dance classes. I couldn't seem to stop myself. Whenever my mind was idle it seemed to always wander to the letter and figuring out who might have left it.

Quickly folding it, I placed it in my jeans pocket and smiled. "Nothing."

"Reeeallly?"

I let out a nervous. "Yes, really."

Her wide pink lips pursed. "I'm calling bullshit. Is it a love note?" Her eyes were bright at the prospect of a secret love affair. My cheeks were flushed even though it was the farthest thing from it.

Now I really did giggle nervously. "Hell no. You know no one on this island likes me but you."

She quirked an eyebrow at me. "Bullshit. Again. And Braden really likes you." She made some kissy noises that made me even redder and I laughed.

I shook my head, confounded. "I don't even understand that."

She pulled her blond hair into a ponytail. "What's not to understand? You're gorgeous and smart."

She said that like I'd always been gorgeous and popular, and everyone knew it. That wasn't the case. I'd never been one of the cool kids here. And not a damn kid at our school cared how academic I was. Until last week, that is. Now Braden seemed to notice me a little too much. I had no idea why or how this was happening all of a sudden. I just knew I wanted it to stop.

I gave Mel's shoulder a nudge with mine. "You don't suck either. But still, I don't get it. He's never shown interest before," I said, sliding on a pair of heels.

She glanced down at my breasts. "It could be the

twins. They seemed to really come in this past summer."

I glanced down at them. She wasn't lying. I'd gone from almost flat-chested to full-on Pamela Anderson in a short four months. I was a late bloomer but a bloomer nonetheless. Unfortunately.

I pulled the front of my shirt away from my breasts, trying to make room in it for those bad boys and nodded at Mel. "It could definitely be the twins."

"Girls," Ms. Donnelly said from the middle of her living room. All of the furniture had been pushed to the corners and she was standing in the middle in a pink monstrosity I'm sure she considered a dress. The pink heels almost made my eyes roll but honestly, I was used to it. This was the same getup as last week.

"Pair up!" Her eyes darted to me and Mel. "Not you two. Find other partners."

Jesus, but that woman hated us.

I paired up with Olivia Drake. She was like a perfect robot child, so I had a blast. Not.

After class, I walked home alone since Mel's mom picked her up to go to dinner. I was salty as hell and I didn't know why. Maybe because of the talk about Braden. Maybe because of the twins. Or maybe because of the debutante classes I was just downright sick of. But I knew it wasn't any of those things. I knew it was because I wanted more than to just examine that note. I wanted to go back out there. To the field. To see if the Coke bottle was still there. It was dangerous, but I was so curious.

Curiosity killed the cat, Liv, I gave myself that pep

42

talk the whole way home. And again later in my room as I lay on the bed with Harry. And when the stars rose in the sky I felt like I was beyond jittery. I tried not to think about the note in the bottle or the field even though I loved it there. It was the last place I'd spent meaningful time with my daddy. But I knew I didn't need to go out there to talk to him now. I could talk to him right here from my bedroom.

Still, I grabbed my blanket and Harry's leash and I was gone. I was practically running down the street and across the bridge. It was humid and sweat poured down my brow and pooled at the small of my back. Harry panted and I worried he might get too hot and I hadn't brought water, so I slowed even though the anticipation damn near killed me.

Finally, we entered the field and Harry and I ran to our spot. I didn't lay out the blanket, but I did push my hand into my pocket to feel for the letter from the last time I'd been here. Knowing it was safe, I searched for the clear Coke bottle in the area I'd found it before, but-terflies in my belly, goose bumps on my skin.

And if I thought for one second that I had belly flut-ters before, I was wrong because when I saw that bottle sitting there with another piece of paper in it, it wasn't just butterflies. It felt like birds.

I raced forward, almost too scared to touch the old glass bottle, but unable not to. I had to know. I picked it up carefully, like it was precious and not just some old discolored bottle in a field.

I slid my pointer finger inside, Harry's leash long

forgotten on the ground. But I never worried about him. He stayed with me always. That leash was there more for the comfort and reassurance of others. My finger brushed the paper and I felt a spark of something. Something that felt bigger than me. Maybe bigger than the stars. It was more than excitement. It was like coming alive. It was electric and it lit me up from the inside until I felt like all of the stars above my head were suddenly all living inside of me.

The note slipped out and into my hand and I looked around the dark field again, desperate to see who had left it here.

Harry lay down on my foot while I unfolded the note. I don't know what I was expecting, but it wasn't what I saw.

Luna,

It's a very clear night, so find the brightest star in the night sky. That bright star, Sirius, is the head of Canis Major Constellation. It almost looks like a stick figure. Can you see it?

I looked up for the brightest star in the sky and sure enough if I followed it down, it looked like it had a body with arms and legs. I smiled at the sky before looking back down at the note.

Canis Major represents the famed Greek dog Laelaps. There are a few origin stories, but the common theme is that he was so fast he was elevated to the skies by Zeus.

Laelaps is also considered to be one of Orion's hunting dogs, trailing behind him in the night sky in pursuit of Taurus the bull, much like your dog trails after you.

Until next time I see you beneath the stars.

That was it? Nothing else? Not a name or a hint? It was the same scribbly writing as before on the same kind of notebook paper. And now I was completely convinced it had to be for me. He'd referenced my dog, for goodness' sake. Was he watching me? But he'd said Luna.

I whipped my cell phone out of my pocket, beyond frustrated, the excitement I'd originally felt ebbing. I pulled up my web browser and Googled the hell out of Luna.

Luna commonly refers to: Earth›s Moon · **Luna** (goddess), the ancient Roman divine personification of the Moon.

The moon? A goddess? But something to do with the moon? I wanted answers.

"Are you there?" I called out into the dark. "Hello!" I spun in circles in the field. What kind of game was this person playing? For a second I thought maybe it was Braden or Sebastian and that thought made me sick. What if this was all just a big joke at my expense? Or maybe it was the guy from the other night. The one who'd tried to get Boone away from me.

I half expected the blond guy to pop out at me any

moment and be like "Gotcha!" But that never happened.

I looked back up at Canis Major, but I didn't smile this time. For once, I didn't want to look at the damn stars. I wanted to know who was doing this. I wanted to know where they were. When they left the damn note. I had approximately five thousand questions and no one to answer them. I was beyond frustrated. So, I snatched up my blanket and grabbed Harry's leash and got the heck out of there. I could admit that I was irrationally pissed at the mystery person who was leaving the notes. I wanted to know why! I wanted to know how!

I stomped like an angry child all the way back to the house, which required more energy than I realized. I was tired when I came upon the mansion, so I didn't notice the police cruiser in the driveway. So, when I opened the door and saw Sheriff Rothchild in the foyer I paused, stunned. It was late. Why was he here?

"Ms. Montgomery!" He smiled at me like it wasn't 10:00 p.m. and he wasn't standing inside my house.

I gave him a weak smile. "Hey, Sheriff. Something wrong?" In my opinion, the law didn't show up for late night calls unless something was terribly wrong. And I didn't see anything alarming.

Georgina's heels clacked against the tile as she entered the foyer and shot me a smile through red lipstick that was too sweet. "Not at all, Livingston. The sheriff was just stopping by to talk some business with me. You know I'm planning a fundraiser for the police department."

She looked too good for 10:00 p.m. Her bleach

blond hair was perfectly coifed, her makeup flawless. Her black slim-fitting dress didn't have a wrinkle to be seen.

And I didn't give a hoot what she did or didn't do with her free time especially for a police department. Hell, I didn't even see why the police department would need a fundraiser. Sheriff Rothchild himself was loaded. Everyone was here.

I looked back at the sheriff and he gave me a wink and a smile that reminded me all too much of Braden. It shouldn't be a surprise since Sheriff Rothchild was Braden's dad. They looked a lot alike and some of their mannerisms were so alike it was downright scary especially since Braden only lived with the sheriff on the weekends from what I heard. His parents had been divorced for as long as I'd been on the island at least.

The sheriff looked me and Harry over. The blanket under my arm drew his attention. "You're out late for a school night." His tone was all at once accusatory and questioning, but I wouldn't feed into it. It wasn't his business what I did, so I just smiled.

"It is very late," Georgina piped in. "I hope you didn't miss your lessons this afternoon."

"No, ma'am," I answered her while letting Harry off his leash.

Flipping her hair over her shoulder, she nodded. "Good girl. I'm just going to walk the sheriff out."

I rolled my eyes. That woman didn't give a crap what I did as long as I did the things she wanted me to. She didn't care how late I was out or who I dated.

Not that I did. Or where I went as long as I didn't miss the classes or social events she wanted me to attend. She was a great example of stellar parenting.

"Night, Livingston," the sheriff called over his shoulder as I made my way to the stairs.

I gave him a quick wave over my shoulder and darted up the steps and through my bedroom door, my hand already in my pocket.

I pulled the letters out and unfolded them both, holding them in my hands. And even though I was still mad at this mystery person, I'd never forget how they felt. They frustrated me. But more than that, they scared the hell out of me. And not because I had a random stranger leaving me notes in a bottle in a field. That fact should have frightened me, but it didn't. Because my life here on the island frightened me more. No, those letters, they felt an awful lot like dreams on paper. Even if they were only directions on where to look in the sky to see the magic of the stars. They seemed like more. Like maybe my daddy who had told me to look up had left them there for me to find. I knew that wasn't the case. So, I could only believe he'd sent someone to me instead. Someone who would get me through. Someone who gave me something so scary, my hands trembled around the papers. Hope.

CHAPTER 6

Adam

Jesus, I was turning into an eerie stalking ass motherfucker, but still I came back time and time again, unable to stay away for one single day. And I watched her. It had started with that one note in a bottle. I knew it was a special night. I myself would be looking at Mars that night and for some stupid reason I couldn't bear her missing it. And now I couldn't bear missing her.

Sometimes she would stare into the distance, get pissed off and yell at the top of her lungs. And I'd laugh because she was fucking cute. She'd stomp off and leave and I'd be sad to see her go, but at least I knew she was headed to the safety of her home and not lying there in a field, begging for trouble.

Other nights she'd read my note and lie underneath the stars and look at what planets or constellations were visible that night. Sometimes the nights were too cloud covered to see the stars and so I left the bottle empty of notes. Sometimes the stars looked so close that I thought maybe I could touch them and I'd leave her a constellation to look at on a ripped piece of notebook paper in that bottle. Yes, every night varied depending on the visibility, but one thing remained the same. Me. I always came and I always watched. On and on it went for weeks and I left more notes and more notes, signing each one with my signature *see you next time beneath the stars*. It was cheesy and hokey, but I didn't give a fuck. I wanted to watch that girl smile through the lenses of my binoculars and so I did. I wanted to make sure she was safe. It worried me that she came alone. It worried me that she came here instead of her home.

Something told me this girl needed someone to make her smile and to take care of her and I'd vowed ten years ago I'd never let anyone down again who needed me. She may have run scared at first, but now she couldn't seem to get enough and I couldn't seem to get enough of her. I rushed here every night. My pops had commented on my absence more than once. Even Raven had noticed I hadn't been around much lately. I was scared of what it said about me that I'd rather be watching her than see my friends and family.

Luna, I called her like the moon. Because I couldn't get the image of her in that dress out of my mind. Her, all milky white with a long white dress on, lying in that field looking like the moon against the stars.

I hid in the tall grass and behind a single tree a hundred yards away and watched as she opened my letters, a small grin on her face, and then I gazed on as she looked at the stars. She talked to herself, the dog, and even closed her eyes and just lay there and I was addicted. Like a drug addict promising only one more hit, I came back day after day, telling myself it would be my last. I knew it was a lie. I couldn't stop. But I also wasn't good with words on the spot. I never had been. I'd always been the quiet, reserved type. These letters were the craziest, outgoing thing I'd ever done that wasn't purely selfish. And I didn't know how to stop and I realized how creepy that was. I really did. But the more I watched her, the less I cared. I just wanted to be near her.

CHAPTER 7

Adam

I'd done a lot of things in my life that weren't very smart at all. Robbing convenience stores. Stealing cigarettes and alcohol. Cheating on tests. Skipping school. Taking drugs. Not kissing my mother before school the last day I'd seen her alive. I'd done it all, but for some reason as I followed the girl from the field and across the bridge this felt like the most stupid thing of all the stupid things.

Somehow, I knew even then that I was way over my head and not just because I was following and essentially stalking someone. Or not even the fact Sheriff Rothchild hated my ass and was basically looking for any reason to throw me in jail. No, those weren't the things that gave me pause when I finally reached the island side of the bridge. No, it was her. The nameless girl who watched the stars. Two weeks of watching her and I was hooked. What would happen when I knew where she lived? What her name was? And God, I wanted to know everything. I wanted to know it all. Favorite colors, foods she loved, why she lay in that field. I wanted to know what her voice sounded like. How old she was. Because fuck if she didn't look a little too young. I wanted all those things. It felt like my brain might explode with all the stuff I wanted to ask her. And that, that was the scary thing. I wanted too much. That too much was all things I knew weren't for me. So, I'd stayed away. Until now, that was. And that's why I knew this was dumb as fuck.

Still, I followed her home like a dumbass. I made sure to keep my eyes peeled for Sheriff Asshole and to stay far enough back that she couldn't see me. I'd spent most of my life hiding, but the last fourteen days had been a true exercise in it and I felt like a damn professional. Ten minutes from the bridge we arrived at her home on the beach. I mean, these people might call it a home, but I called it a mansion. She walked in with her dog and I stood on the sidewalk in front of the house, staring. I noticed on the way home, I liked the way she walked. It wasn't a stroll or even a fast-paced jaunt. No, she walked on the tips of her toes and almost never used her heels. It was adorable and almost reminded me of a slow skip.

I knew she was rich. I could tell from her clothes and from the sheer fact that she was from the island, but this blew my mind. I looked over the expensive cars in the driveway, my feet moving closer and into her front yard almost unbeknownst to me. I was eating up every little bit of information I could. Her address, the color of her house, when I heard the telltale whine of a door opening and then I knew I was truly fucked. So very fucked because I couldn't move. I felt glued to the spot waiting, almost anticipating this moment. It was like I came here to do this. And maybe I had. It was like I couldn't wait one more day to be closer to her. I was a fool.

The jangle of a dog's collar followed by footsteps and there she stood, the closest she'd ever been to me besides that day with Boone and Grady. There she was, too skinny legs, too wide mouth and all. I was starting to like that mouth that looked like it held too many teeth. She wore black leggings and an oversized T-shirt. My mouth went dry and I ran a hand through my hair, but I couldn't make myself move. My heart raced in my chest, my breath came fast.

She kept moving toward me until she stood at the top of the driveway and I stood at the bottom. Her feet were bare and her hair was down, blowing in the salty breeze coming off the ocean, and her eyes—they were on me.

She squinted a bit at me as her dog sat down next to her feet. Some protection he was. I looked on, afraid to move. I wanted to watch her from this close up and I knew what kind of crazy that spoke about me, but I didn't fucking care.

I felt like we were in some sort of weird, twisted stare down until she finally spoke. "You." It was said on a breath of disbelief and accusation.

It wasn't a question and I wasn't a big talker, so I just stood there, staring like the fool I was.

She stepped closer slowly, her dog at her heels until she was all the way down the driveway and standing not a foot in front of me. My heart thundered in my chest. I wasn't a stalker really, but I had a feeling that tonight might be the first time in the history of my life that someone was about to call me one.

Her forehead scrunched as she looked me over. "Did you follow me here? From the field?" She bit her lip nervously. I wanted to touch my finger to it, beg her not to hurt that mouth I was growing to like.

But instead, I nodded, lost for words, letting her deep, almost sultry voice wash over me. Her voice wasn't all like I expected and oh, had I expected. Because I'd thought of this girl more than I cared to admit. So, I paid attention, waiting for her next words, but all I could hear was the thundering in my heart.

This was a mistake, but it was one I was powerless to stop.

Her brown eyes glazed over in thought and then snapped back to mine. "Wait. So you..." Her finger pointed at me. "You...Oh my God. *You've* been leaving me the notes?" Her words were incredulous, but no one was as shocked as me at the shit I'd been doing the last couple of weeks.

I nodded again, lifting my hand and looking for the tiny line on my forehead that Raven had told me about. I pressed the line, pissed off. Why was she so surprised it was me? Who the hell did she think it was? I was irrationally pissed off about some other dude stalking this chick and I didn't even know her name. I was insane.

I reached in my pocket for a cigarette and a lighter, hoping like hell the nicotine would calm me the hell down.

"But I thought it was…" Her voice trailed off as I lit my cigarette.

I raised an eyebrow as an indication that she should keep going and tell me who the hell she thought had been watching her and leaving her notes. Because I was probably going to kill this man.

But instead she stepped back and pointed at me again. "Are you smoking?" Her lip curled in disgust.

I nodded again.

It was her turn to look disgusted this time. "Do you even speak?"

I nodded again and she shook her head in disbelief before reaching over the space between us and snatching the cigarette out of my mouth so fast I didn't see it coming. I stood there dumbfounded. People didn't snatch shit away from me. People were scared of me. Not this brave girl. I should have known.

"Smoking is disgusting." She said it quietly like it didn't matter, but I could tell it did to her. She bent over and put the butt out on the driveway before standing up again and shoving it in her pocket.

I smirked. "You gonna keep that?"

Her eyes ignited with anger. "No, I'm going to throw it in the trash because I'm not a litterbug."

Shaking my head, I muttered under my breath, "Fucking litterbug." She was being cute. The girl with the too long legs and too big mouth that I couldn't get out of my mind was fucking cute, too. I was screwed.

I wanted to full-on smile at her cuteness, but I held my happiness close to my chest. God knew it always came with a price. And I was done paying.

"You kiss your momma with that smoke mouth?" she asked snarkily, clearly pissed off about my smirk.

I lowered my head and took a step back, running a hand through my dark hair. I wanted to tell this girl things. Things I had no business telling her, like that I didn't kiss my momma with anything anymore. Instead, I asked the question that had been plaguing me since she'd seemed surprised it was me who had left the notes.

"Who did you think it was?"

Her face screwed up in confusion. "What?"

I stood straighter and licked my lips before answering. "Who did you think left the notes?"

I was feeling strangely vulnerable in that moment waiting for her answer and I didn't like it one bit. Why did it matter to me who wrote her or didn't? Or who else thought she was the most intriguing thing ever? For fuck's sake, she was just another rich bitch from the island. Why did anything about what she was about to say matter to me at all?

She bit her lip again and I still wanted to reach over and pull it from her teeth. It was sexy that lip bite, innocent even, and for some reason that made it all the more attractive.

"I don't know." Her brow furrowed in thought and she looked away, almost like she didn't want to tell me the answer to my question. But then her eyes landed on mine again. "I thought it was the other guy—"

"Boone?" I interrupted loudly.

A disgusted look crossed her face. "God, no. Not him. The blond. The other guy."

I let out a long breath accompanied by a sarcastic chuckle. "Grady?" That guy didn't even graduate high school and she thought he knew anything about astronomy. I would have laughed if the whole thing hadn't annoyed me so much.

Her eyes brightened. "Is that his name?"

I pulled out my pack of cigarettes again. "You like him or something?"

"What? No!"

I walked out into the street and lit my smoke far away from her.

She started to follow me. "Where are you going?"

"Home."

"But I don't even know your name!" she yelled and stomped a foot.

I almost smiled again.

I turned and started walking back toward the bridge. I didn't know hers either and I wanted to ask for it, but it was enough for now that I knew where she lived, what her voice sounded like, and the faces she made when she was pissed.

I'd take the things I did find out and leave before she made me kill one of my oldest friends.

"Next time," I called out, trying my damnedest not to look back. I didn't want to give her the satisfaction of knowing what she did to me. Not when she thought

Grady had left her the damn notes. It didn't surprise me. He was the one who'd tried to get Boone to leave her alone, but fuck, it had been me who had ultimately stopped it. It had been me who watched her every night. It had been me who told her about the stars. Fucking Grady.

I was rolling my eyes when I heard her yell from behind me. "Tomorrow! You'll tell me tomorrow."

CHAPTER 8

Liv

"**L**iv, did you hear me? Liv!"

My eyes shot to Mel's and left my view of the ocean. "Sorry," I panted out, from next to her as we ran the length of the beach.

It was the weekend and we'd gotten up early to get a run in mostly because our parents insisted on it. Can't be chubby at your coming out party. *Eye roll.* Mel had been going on and on about some guy she met at a party the other night, but I'd been a terrible friend because all I could think about was last night.

And even though I'd been staring out at the beautiful sunrise over the Carolina beach, I hadn't noticed it at all. No, I was still back in the driveway, barefoot and with the tattooed guy standing in front of me. Imagine my shock. I never dreamed for one moment it was him leaving me the notes. Mostly because the person who left me notes knew a lot about the stars and that guy? He didn't look like he knew much about anything except for how to get in trouble.

But it was him. Stingingly cold blue eyes and all. He'd been standing there looking too damn beautiful in the twilight. I didn't know what had possessed me to walk back outside that night. I'd just known, had a feeling deep inside me. Those colorful tattoos standing out against his skin like tiny paintings on the plain white wall of a museum. His dark hair too long, his eyes eating me up.

I finally met him and he'd followed me home and he'd stood there seemingly lost at first and then angry all of a sudden. And me, I'd been different. I'd felt safe with him. I'd snatched that cigarette out of his gorgeous mouth and demanded a name. I smiled as I remembered myself in that moment. Brave. I'd been a badass.

"What are you over there mooning about?"

Wiping the sweat from my forehead, I panted out, "Nothing."

I wouldn't be telling anyone about tattoo boy. No, he was my secret to keep. Besides if Georgina caught wind of him there would be hell to pay. Those tattoos and bad boy attitude weren't exactly her cup of tea. It wasn't that I didn't want to tell Mel. It was more a matter of couldn't. I wanted to lay it all out there for her. This was one of the most exciting things that had ever happened to me. Of course I wanted to share it with her, but I knew better.

She came to a dead stop and bent over at the waist, trying to catch her breath. Her blue eyes sparkled up at me. "You've met someone."

I laughed nervously and continued jogging in place

like she didn't totally have me pegged. "What? No! You're crazy!"

"No, I'm not," she said, sitting up and stretching her legs. "You never get moony-eyed. But you totally are right now. You've been daydreaming all morning."

Denial wasn't just a river in Egypt anymore. "No way. I'd never date anyone from the island. And you know it."

Her eyebrows took flight right to her hairline. "Ah, but did you meet someone who wasn't from the island?"

My face got hot. "No. There's no one. I was just thinking about schoolwork and etiquette classes and the stupid debutante ball coming up. I'm overwhelmed, not in love, crazy lady!"

She started a slow walk back to the house and I fell in step with her.

"I didn't say you were in love. I said you met someone."

"You're wrong." If you were gonna lie, then you had to stick to it.

The look she threw told me she knew I was full of shit, so I just smiled and batted my eyelashes. That move had saved Southern girls for centuries.

"Fine. Don't tell me about lover boy."

I pursed my lips before throwing back, "How do you know it's not lover girl?" I licked my lips and her eyes fell to them.

Her eyes went wide. "Oh my God! Is it?"

I stopped on the beach so I could double over in laughter. "Come on, Mel," I said through my giggles.

"You've known me for years. You don't think I would have mentioned that I was a lesbian?"

She threw her hands up in the air. "How the hell am I supposed to know? You're like the Fort Knox of secrets over there. You hold everything so damn close to your chest."

Her face was red and she'd crossed her arms over her breasts. I'd known Mel long enough to know when she was getting pissed, but still I kept laughing until she finally leaned forward so we were eye to eye. "You're a dick, Livingston Montgomery!" Her ponytail swung out as she turned around and started stomping down the beach.

I smiled as I yelled out, "No! But I do, however, like dick!"

I'd never had a dick in my life, so I didn't know how much I liked it or not, but I just couldn't miss the opportunity to give Mel a hard time.

She paused long enough to shoot me a look over her shoulder while calling out, "Hilarious."

I jogged to catch up to her, still chuckling quietly. I pulled her swinging ponytail. "Don't be mad, Mel. I was only joking."

She gave me some side-eye action and tried to hold back a smile. "I know. But you're still a dick."

I nodded. "I am. Forgive me?"

"I'll think about it."

"Good. I can't have the only person in all of Saint Ashley who actually likes me mad at me."

She rolled her eyes. "You're so dramatic. I am not

the only person who likes you."

"You totally are," I deadpanned.

"Braden likes you."

"Braden likes anyone with a vagina, Mel. That hardly counts."

She nudged my shoulder with hers. "You should give him a chance. He's a good guy, has money, and his daddy is the sheriff."

I didn't tell Mel that those qualities meant diddly squat to me. No, I wanted a man who thought I'd hung the moon. I wanted a man who loved me. I just wanted a man. Not a boy who only considered himself important because of his social status. Love couldn't be measured in dollars.

We reached my house just in time to avoid any more talk of Braden, so I waved Mel off and headed toward my house, thankful for the weekend where etiquette classes and school were nonexistent. And even though I didn't usually go to the field on the weekends, I would tonight because I'd told him tomorrow and it was finally tomorrow. It had been a long wait all night in my bed imagining what his name could be. Imagining what he might say to me. I'd hardly slept a wink at all.

I was daydreaming about tattoo boy again while I reached into the fridge to grab a cold bottle of water. I turned around and closed the fridge and ran straight into a hard body.

"Oomph." My water bottle rolled across the floor and Sebastian leaned over and grabbed it.

I stood there, staring at him as he blocked the exit

to the kitchen. I held my hand out, hoping he'd hand over the water bottle but knowing all too well the kind of shit my stepbrother normally did.

He didn't hold the bottle out but instead kept it in his fist right at his side. "Come get it, Livingston."

So, I did. I leaned over far enough that I didn't have to walk a foot to get close to him and snatched the bottle out of his hand.

"Can you move out of the way?" I ground out, my hand tight around the water bottle.

He nodded. "Sure."

I started forward, but he still blocked my way, so I backed up, determined to not get close enough that he could do something creepy like smell me or whisper in my ear. My skin crawled at the thought.

He smiled and I felt sick. He always did this. Pretended to be amicable and then delivered a killer blow. "I'll move. As soon as you tell me where you've been going every fucking night."

I swallowed. Terrified he knew. Terrified he'd followed me. I thought I'd been careful. Always making sure he wasn't home or waiting until everyone was tucked into their beds. I realized now how wrong I'd been. Sebastian was always watching me. Always waiting for a weak moment to attack. Always looking for a way in.

I shrugged my shoulders and looked at the floor. I was a terrible liar, but I'd lie until the cows came home about this. There was no way in hell I was telling Sebastian about my daddy's field. About the notes.

About my tattooed boy waiting there for me.

My head swam. How would I get out tonight? Would he be watching and waiting for me to leave? Would he follow me across the bridge and ruin the one place I had left? Ruin my chance to finally talk to the boy who'd revealed himself?

"I've been having trouble sleeping." I kicked at the tiled floor with my tennis shoe and more sweat pooled at the bottom of my back. I felt like I was under a heating lamp instead of Sebastian's watchful stare. "I sometimes walk to the beach. I think it's the stress of the ball coming up. Of all the classes with Ms. Donnelly."

I looked up at him through my eyelashes briefly to gauge whether he believed my lie. His lips were pursed like he was in thought and I had a brief second where I thought I would get off scot-free.

"By yourself?"

I looked up at him, stunned by his question. He'd warned away all the boys at school. Who did he think I was taking long walks with?

"Yeah. By myself," I said quietly, so sick and tired of this. So done with being worried about Sebastian. So over the interrogations and intimidations. So sick of being worried constantly. So tired of walking on eggshells.

"Mmm," he rumbled out, his brown eyes thoughtful, his stature intimidating the hell out of me. Sebastian was big and strong and smart. He was a deadly combination when he wanted to be. But he must have decided to cut me some slack today because he moved to the side and I didn't waste a second wondering why as

I rushed past and straight to the shower. I locked the hell out of that door and while I showered, I thought about how being careful wasn't good enough anymore. He was on to me. I couldn't risk him finding my field, my notes about the stars, or my tattooed boy. He'd take them all away from me as brutally as possible and I couldn't risk that.

I finished bathing just in time to join stepmonster and evil stepbrother for dinner. It was silent as we ate, but Sebastian's eyes were forever watchful. They rarely left me, even as he cut his steak.

I gave a big yawn at the end of the meal, claiming I was exhausted, and headed to bed. Harry and I climbed the steps and I turned off the lights and slipped under the covers with my cell phone, Harry warming my feet at the bottom of the bed. I watched YouTube videos on my cell phone until late, making sure everyone in the house was asleep, especially crazy ass Sebastian.

I didn't take Harry. I was scared his toenails across the tile would wake someone, so it was just me and my blue blanket as I stole off into the night.

Praying the tattooed boy was still there waiting for me, I jogged across the bridge in my black yoga pants and Saint Ashley Prep T-shirt, my blue flip-flops pinching between my toes. I whipped through the grass like lightning, excitement spurring me on when I came to my spot in the field. I'd waited later to make sure I knew everyone was completely asleep. I gazed around, looking for my Coke bottle, but more importantly searching for the boy.

Nothing. No Coke bottle. No letter. Nothing. And the clouds were so thick tonight, there weren't even any stars. I could have cried.

"Helloooo," I called out but was only greeted by silence.

My breathing became labored and my heart felt like it was pounding out of my chest. Oh my God. It was over. He wasn't here. He'd left me no notes. We were done. He was done with me after last night. I was pretty sure this was what having a panic attack was. I didn't know why I was so devastated. I'd just met him, but I think that was mostly the reason I was so sad. I didn't get to know his name, why he left the notes, how he knew so much about the stars.

The prickle of tears burned my eyes as I threw the blue blanket on the ground haphazardly and sat down. I was beyond disappointed. I buried my face in my hands, trying to hold back the tears. I was stupid. Why had I gotten my hopes up about some tattooed bad boy? It was so unlike me. But he'd tricked me. He'd tricked me with the stars and the romantic notes and the freakin' Coke bot—

"You're late." A deep voice snapped me out of wallowing.

I looked up through blurry eyes and there he stood, the source of all my sadness. God, he looked good and not just because I was so relieved to see him. He was standing right over me, but still I could see the muscles underneath his tight white T-shirt that fed into tight dark jeans. My eyes devoured him like he was their favorite snack. I got all the way down to black boots that looked like Doc Martin knockoffs and I was practically swooning. He was intimidating as hell, but God, he was beautiful. My eyes swept back up his body and to the tattoos that poked out of the top of his T-shirt and onto his neck. And that jaw. It was hard and square—unyielding. I wanted to touch it. And then my eyes hit ice-cold blue ones. They weren't smiling. They weren't friendly, but still my stomach somersaulted as I took them in. His black hair was messy, like he hadn't brushed it in a while, but it didn't matter. It was perfect just the way it was.

He was the quintessential bad boy, but everything about him was just too damn good.

I couldn't look away, which was probably why he finally asked, "Are you gonna move over or what?"

"Oh," I mumbled stunned and dazed, scooting over on the blue blanket to make room.

As he was sitting down my mind suddenly cleared. "Wait!" I shouted.

He went from a crouching position to standing straight up again beside me. "What?" He looked startled.

And even though part of me was feeling starstruck, I wouldn't let him be another person in my life who controlled me or railroaded over me.

I looked toward the blue blanket. "You gotta give me a name before you sit on my daddy's blanket, tattoo boy."

He quirked a dangerously dark eyebrow down at

me. "Tattoo boy?"

I said one word back, giving him big eyes, because he had to be kidding me. He had nicknames for me, too. "Luna?"

He nodded thoughtfully before answering. "Adam. Adam Nova."

I blinked, not quite believing it. "Nova?"

Like the star. A star that burned bright until it burned out. I was pretty sure that was what a nova was. It seemed highly unlikely that a boy who knew about the stars had a last name like that. He had to be full of shit.

"Yep," he said, sitting down next to me like we'd done this my entire life. Like it wasn't a big deal. Like butterflies weren't swarming my belly. Like this wasn't the most epic event of my teenage life.

"You're joking?"

"Nope."

What the hell? I wanted to know more. How did a guy who knew about the stars have a last name like Nova? "Are you going to elaborate?"

"Nope," he mumbled as he reclined back until he was looking at the cloud-covered sky.

I lay next to him. It was as awkward as you can imagine. I was stiff and scared, just a sixteen-year-old girl who'd never even kissed a boy, much less lain next to one on a blanket beneath the stars.

So, I did what I normally did when I felt embarrassed or awkward. I talked because I was one of those who couldn't help it. "Don't you wanna know mine?"

His head slowly turned in my direction and once again those blue eyes were on me, making me shiver and feel like I was full of fire simultaneously. "Wanna know what?"

His voice said that he didn't care what the hell I was talking about, but those eyes told a different story. Those eyes said he couldn't get enough of me.

I scoffed at his question. "My name."

He scooted over so he was closer to me. "Of course."

Oh. My. God. Did Adam Nova ever have a normal conversation in his entire life or were they all like this— overcomplicated as hell. Jesus, if he could just articulate one freaking thought it would be awesome.

"Then why didn't you ask?"

He shrugged. "I figured you were going to tell me."

"When do you leave the notes?"

His face was back to the sky. "As soon as it gets dark out."

"And then what?"

"And then I wait."

"Why?"

"I don't know," he said to the clouds.

"And when I finally get here? What then?"

He blew out a long breath and then fell quiet. I thought maybe he wasn't going to answer me, but his voice and what he said shocked me. "I watched."

You could have knocked me over with a feather and I was already lying on the dang ground. My jaw worked as I stumbled over my next words. "Why?"

His head seemed to turn in slow motion as his eyes

71

collided with mine like two semis wrecking head-on. "Because I couldn't *not* watch."

Goose bumps broke out on my skin and I felt my chest tighten. I couldn't describe what I felt in that moment. I felt scared. I felt excited. And flattered. No one watched me, but Sebastian. No one really cared but my creepy stepbrother and for the wrong reasons. And while Adam was odd in his own right something told me he was safe. I lay there on the blanket, staring at the sky in awe, in shock. He'd watched me. He'd put tiny notes in a bottle and watched me open them and then he'd lain here in this very spot and stargazed. Why? *Because he couldn't not watch me.* I couldn't wrap my head around it.

"Are you gonna tell me or what?"

I snapped out of my daze and turned to look at him, but he was back to looking up at the sky. "Tell you what?"

"Your name," he whispered.

I felt myself smile. He wanted to know it, even though he hadn't asked. I wanted to know a million things about him myself, but I knew he'd be a tough nut to crack. So, I did what any teenage girl who liked a boy did. I played hard to get. And boy was I playing because I was already got.

"Tomorrow."

CHAPTER 9

Adam

It was tomorrow. And I was excited about it. And that probably wasn't a good thing. I floated through the morning high on whatever pheromones the girl I called Luna had put off yesterday. The girl was like a drug. I practically fucking skipped to work this morning. It was ridiculous and still I couldn't stop thinking about her no matter how hard I tried. So, I'd left work and come to my afternoon classes and sat through them not hearing a damn word. It was a good thing my grades were good because I knew there would be plenty of days ahead of me that I'd be sitting here thinking of that moment. The one where I told her the truth. The truth that I really hadn't even admitted to myself yet. *Because I can't not watch.*

What was wrong with me? I never got this worked up over anything or anyone. It was so out of character, so different for me. I couldn't stop myself from going to her, from being with her. I didn't want to.

God, our faces had been so close together that

night all I had to do was lean forward and my mouth would have been on hers. Her molten eyes had spoken volumes in those seconds after I'd made my confession and they didn't say the things I thought they would. She wasn't angry or scared, or upset.

I'd lain back stunned, wondering if anything at all ever scared that fearless girl.

"Mr. Nova, please stay after class," Professor Johnson interrupted my thoughts.

English class was over and everyone was getting up to leave and there I was still daydreaming about a girl whose name I didn't know.

The girl beside me walked by and made sure to run her hand down the length of my tattooed arm. "Nice tats," she murmured seductively before giving me the look. The one that said you can meet me in my car in the parking lot and have me in the back seat. I got those looks a lot. They didn't interest me. I didn't have the time or inclination for random hookups anymore.

Grabbing my bag, I got up and walked through the classroom, ignoring the girl and knowing I was going to get the lecture of the century for not paying attention in class.

"Have a seat, Adam." He pointed me toward the seat right in front of the classroom and grabbed some papers off his desk.

Curious what was happening, I sat down, watching him. He turned toward me and placed something on my desk. With furrowed brow, I looked at the paper. It was mine. The same paper I'd turned in only days ago.

He sat at the desk next to mine and pointed at the paper. "We need to talk about that paper."

"Okay," I replied and I knew how I came off—aloof. I wore my nonchalance like a damn armor. It was the only way I knew how to be.

"It's brilliant. Your work on this one is amazing. The way you used chemistry and mathematics to describe the evolution of the stars and planets—"

"Jesus, not this again, Prof. It's a damn English class." I stood up, ready to get the hell out of there because I knew what was coming. Teachers at technical weren't supposed to care so damn much, but this one did, and as much as it flattered me and fed my ego it got on my nerves because he could never understand my circumstances.

He stood up and followed me, right on my heels as I headed toward the door. "Come on, Adam. You know the English is good. And I know, I'm just an amateur astronomer, but you, son, you're something more. You don't belong at some dinky tech school."

I stopped and spun on a heel until we were face-to-face and lied like hell. "I like it here."

Couldn't he just leave me alone? It wasn't like I had a choice. I was just going here to get my basic classes and hoped to one day have enough money to attend a university close by.

He shook his head. "Bullshit, Adam. Your high school grades, your grades the past year here, they don't say that you like it here. They say you're fuckin bored. You're a brilliant mind and you belong in one of the best Astronomy & Astrophysics schools in the country. Not rotting away here. Let me help you."

He tried to land a hand to my shoulder, but I shrugged him off and sprinted for the door. "Not interested, Prof," I lied again. I didn't like lying, but it was a hell of a lot easier than the truth. The truth that I couldn't leave my father to fend for himself. Not on his meager disability wages. No, he needed the income from my job as well. This dinky technical school was just going to have to cut it for now. Hell, how about somebody give me some damn credit for going to school at all.

And even though I had a chip on my shoulder the size of Jupiter, I still was excited to head to the field.

Feeling pissed about my circumstances and even more pissed off that the professor kept pushing the issue, I stalked across the grass, exhausted after working all morning and schooling all damn day. It all seemed so monotonous. So never-ending.

Like always, she was there, waiting. Only this time, she was looking for me.

"Hey," she said quietly from the blanket, her dog taking a nap on the ground beside her.

I nodded toward the dog. "Laelaps."

She shook her head on a giggle. "Nope, just plain old Harry."

I sat down next to her, my jean-clad thigh pressed to her naked one. Her shorts were dangerously short.

"And you?"

She pushed her hand out in front of her and I

couldn't do anything but take it. We shook as she said, "Livingston Rose Montgomery at your service." She said it in a thick Southern accent that almost made me smile.

Instead, I lay back on the blanket and looked at the stars, still weary from the day and cranky from class.

"God, today sucked. I freaking hate etiquette classes and I had two today. Two! I mean, how much torture is a sixteen-year-old girl supposed to endure? Being Southern is hard, Nova." She nudged her thigh to mine and I grumbled out an acknowledgment that wasn't a word at all but more a sound.

Sixteen. And I was nineteen. She was too young for me, but I was drawn to her in an explicable way that I couldn't deny.

Already I was feeling better from just being near her. I felt like a weight had been lifted off my shoulders. Like maybe classes at the tech school and taking care of my dad weren't so bad as long as this girl was here at night.

"What do you think this means, Adam?" She was gazing at the stars.

"What means?" I mumbled.

She motioned to the sky with her chin. "This."

My eyes darted to the sky and then to her. "I think it means in the grand scheme of things, we're small, so unimportant. Look how big the universe is." My voice was quiet.

She turned to me slowly, her face serious. "For such small things, we can make a huge difference, though, right?"

I couldn't stand how hopeful her eyes were.

The question burned on my tongue. "Is that what you want to do? Make a difference?"

Gazing at the sky, she answered, "Absolutely."

That was it. That one word, but it said it all. There was no doubt in my mind Livingston would change the world.

She was only quiet a few moments after our exchange and eventually started talking about her school work, her dog, her friend Mel. I heard it all while never uttering a single word. Jesus, the girl could talk. But I didn't want to know about those things. The things I wanted to know were more personal. More hidden.

When she finally quieted and was staring into space herself, I asked the question I'd been wanting her to answer all night.

"Why do you do it?"

Her head snapped over to look at me and her eyes were wide. Her jaw dropped and she pressed a hand to her chest. "Did you"—she pointed at my face—"just actually open your mouth and move it while sounds came out of it?"

I rolled my eyes and laid my head back down with a sigh before turning my head to the side and giving her an eat shit look.

She giggled. "What? You've said all of two words to me. I'm in shock right now. I might keel over and die. The earth is moving under my feet. I feel the sky tumbling down—"

I almost laughed at her ridiculousness. "Isn't that a song?"

"I don't know. Is it?" She grinned, being totally cute and throwing me back into silence.

But I didn't need to talk. God knew she could totally talk enough for both of us.

"Why do I do what?"

"Lie out here all the time? Come to this field when you could stay at your cushy home on the island? Talk to yourself like a maniac?" My questions were fucking endless when it came to Livingston Montgomery. I told myself it was because I was curious. It was a lie. I told myself it was because she was intriguing. It was a lie. No, I couldn't get enough of her. I was obsessed. I wanted to know everything. I wanted to see the stars through her eyes.

Her eyebrows hit her hairline. "A maniac? Wow. I think I liked you better when you didn't say anything. In fact, I think you were best when you just left notes in a glass bottle."

I just stared, waiting on my answers, trying not to let her words wound me. I was quiet, reserved. Someone who really knew me may say shy and socially awkward. Most other people just thought I was an asshole thug. But I shouldn't have asked the questions the way I did. I wasn't good with words or feelings or even people, really. On top of that, I was still grouchy as fuck from class and taking it out on her.

She blew out a long breath and swallowed. "You shouldn't just assume things about people, Adam.

Not everything is always as it seems." She shot me a dirty look. "And you have no idea what my life is like, and trust me, it is far from"—she threw up air quotes—"cushy."

I just stared at her, not knowing what to say mostly because she was right. I shouldn't assume things and part of me felt bad about it, but the smarter part of me knew she was safer over there. On the island. Away from me. And definitely away from this side of town.

Her brow was furrowed and her jaw was clenched. "What are you looking at?" she growled, standing up and crouching next to her side of the blanket. She started to roll up the blanket until she couldn't anymore, because I was still lying on it.

"You can move."

"I know I can."

She pulled on the blanket.

"Get off my blanket, tattoo boy."

"That's mature," I deadpanned.

She pulled on the blanket hard, while her dog danced around her nervously, but I didn't budge or attempt to move. She was actually being kinda cute and I felt myself smirk.

"I don't give a flying fuck if you think I'm mature! I'm sixteen! I can be immature if I want, asshole!" she yelled from above me and my smirk almost became a full-on smile.

"You kiss your mother with that mouth, young lady?"

She paused and stared down at me, her jaw

clenched before she pulled hard on the blanket and sent me rolling into the grass. I cussed as I landed face down on the grass.

She snapped the blanket over me as she continued to roll it. "No, I don't kiss my mother at all, you stupid, jerk face, assuming asshat. I can't because both of my parents are dead and I come out here to talk to them. I come out here for some peace." She stepped over me like a piece of shit she was avoiding getting on her shoe and started speed walking toward the bridge that would take her home.

And I was. I was a big old piece of shit. Jesus, I stuck my foot in it tonight. I wondered to whom she was going home to if both of her parents were dead. And I felt like a dick. A big one. Not because of how I'd spoken to her or the things I'd said. I was just me. And I'd long since given up people's ideals of what they thought I should do or say because I usually said whatever the hell I wanted when I talked. And it was mostly awkward and sometimes not nice, but it was always honest. No, I didn't feel bad about our conversation. I felt bad that she'd lost her parents. I felt bad that she came here and talked to balls of gas and heat, instead of actual people. I felt bad that she, for some reason, felt this place was safer than her home on the island.

"Livingston Rose Montgomery!" I yelled, getting up off the ground. She didn't turn around, but I swore that her dog gave me a dirty ass look. Hell, I deserved it. I didn't feel right chasing her. I thought maybe it would scare her and that was the last thing I wanted. I needed for her to come back like I needed air, but I wouldn't frighten her.

"Livingston!" I shouted louder this time. She didn't turn around or acknowledge me except for the slow rise of her middle finger over her head while she continued to walk with a slow swing to her hips that made me realize she had a great ass.

I chuckled low. She was all heat and fire, that girl. It was a wonder she hadn't already burned me to a crisp. I was already counting down the seconds until I could see her again.

CHAPTER 10

Liv

I could have played it cool. I could have avoided the field and made Adam work for it. It wasn't in me. But I didn't. I couldn't. I found enduring school and etiquette classes during the light somehow wasn't so bad knowing Adam would be there in the dark. And even though he held his cards close to the chest and hardly spoke a word, I felt saved. I felt like I had a purpose. Adam was my purpose all of a sudden. He made it so much easier to get through the days. But I didn't know what that said about me exactly. That a boy I had only known in person a week had that kind of hold over me. It was as scary as it was exhilarating.

I came to the field sometimes not until midnight and made sure to be extra careful when leaving. I'd even taken to walking the beach a little before heading across the bridge to make sure no one was following me. I wouldn't risk Adam. Not when hanging out with him had me so happy the last several days. He wasn't a chatter bug and I was completely okay with that because he was real. There weren't any fake pretenses or niceties between us. I trusted him implicitly because he didn't have anything to gain from our friendship but me. He just valued me and not my money or my inheritance.

Braden, who was still insistent that he take me on a date, hadn't even been able to ruin my good mood. Even Georgina and Sebastian had been scarce lately and that's what I was thinking when a knock sounded at my bedroom door as I was doing my homework. It was like I had conjured them up.

"Yes," I said, not moving from the desk because if it was Sebastian I wasn't opening that door for all the money in the world.

"I'd like to talk with you for a moment, Livingston," Georgina purred from the other side of the door.

I rolled my eyes and took a deep breath, trying to emotionally prepare myself for the conversation. I did this any time she asked if we could talk. Because it was never about anything important to me or really pertaining to anything I cared about. No, the only time Georgina wanted to talk was when she needed something from me. Something that would benefit her.

I pasted the fakest smile ever on my face and opened the door a crack. "Yes?"

She looked from my eyes and down the rest of the crack in the door and back up again before clearing her throat and then saying snidely, "May I come in?"

My odd smile got wider even as my brain nearly exploded. I hated them in my room. This was the only place I could call my own besides the field on the other side of the bridge. But I moved back and swung the door open anyway. I didn't like to piss Georgina off. She had become a crazy person when she was mad ever since my father's death. I'd never been a huge fan of her. Not when they dated. Not when he moved us to this island for her. And definitely not when he married her, but I'd reasoned out that I wouldn't have to put up with her for the rest of my life like him and he seemed to enjoy her company. My not being a huge fan had turned into pretty much hating her face off since he'd died. She'd changed. She'd gone from mildly snotty to full-on crazy town temper tantrums when she didn't get her way.

"What's up?" I asked, nice as pie.

She was wearing an expensive looking gray skirt suit with a pale pink blouse beneath. Her ever present pearls hung from her neck and big diamond studs adorned her ears. Her hair was pulled up in a loose bun. She was way the hell overdressed for 9:00 p.m., but since I'd met her I'd never seen the woman not dressed to the nines. I wasn't even sure she actually owned pajamas.

She sat on my bed and crossed her legs at the ankle, all Southern class. "I wanted to talk to you about the debutante ball coming up in a few months."

I was confused. What did we need to talk about? I was taking all the stupid classes and we'd already ordered my dress.

"Okay?" I stood across the room from her, preparing for the absolutely worst, and I wasn't wrong.

She picked a piece of lint off my comforter and

it made me irrationally mad. "I'd like for you to have Braden escort you."

I sucked in a breath and before I could stop myself, my panic spilled over and right out of my mouth. "What? But why?"

Her back went straight and one perfectly plucked, blond eyebrow shot up and dared me to say anything more.

A saccharine smile hit her lips and she straightened her skirt. I knew this technique. This was Georgina's way of coming up with all the bullshit. It was a stalling tactic until she got all the facts together and ready to go. I'd seen her do it five thousand times to my father and only a hundred or so more to me.

I rolled my eyes and crossed my arms over my chest, feeling beyond defensive. She couldn't tell me who to take to the ball. That should be my choice.

"Braden's a nice boy. He comes from a nice family. His father is the sheriff and I heard he fancies you." She finished the last part in a sing-song voice that made my lip curl and my nose scrunch.

"Oh, stop with the dramatic faces, Livingston. It's not that big of a deal. It's one dance, for heaven's sake."

I couldn't believe it. She was the one sitting there being dramatic about whom I should take to my coming out ball and I hadn't said a word, yet I was being dramatic. I didn't even want to go to the ball. Oh, the absurdity of it all nearly sent me over the edge.

I wouldn't stomp my feet or shout or cry like a teenager. I wouldn't give her the actual pleasure of seeing me be dramatic. So instead, I just calmly asked, "Why can't I ask who I'd like to ask to the ball?"

Her eyes widened in pretend shock while she checked out the manicure on her right hand. "Oh, did you have someone in mind, then?"

I swallowed hard. I did have someone in mind. But he had tattoos and a bit of a bad attitude about 99 percent of the time. And I was pretty sure he was in college and I was still just a junior in high school. Georgina would hate him and the thought almost made me smile. "Maybe," I choked out.

Her eyes were ice on mine. She was starting to get that crazy look in her eyes. The one that usually led to one of her epic mommy dearest meltdowns. "Do tell."

Christ, but I was a complete chicken shit, so I answered, "No one in particular, really, but there are a couple of cute boys I might like to take."

"Well, Braden's cute, too," she sang, standing up and walking over to me. "And I trust him. He's your brother's best friend. He'll take good care of you."

I bet he would. I knew how well he and Sebastian took care of girls.

"It's settled then, yes?" She railroaded over me before I could say more. A firm squeeze to the top of my arm and she was gone, the only evidence of her the slight crease in my comforter and the smell of expensive perfume in the air.

I snatched my comforter straight again and stomped over to my desk. I wasn't going to that damn dance with Braden. I'd leave first. I wouldn't go at all.

I'd let that bitch tell me what to do most of the time, but she didn't get to tell me who I dated. I was taking Adam to that dance if it was the last thing I did or there wouldn't be a cotillion at all.

I hated how Georgina controlled me, but I didn't have a lot of choice until I was an adult and could get the hell out of there. To the other people on the island we were the perfect family. No one suspected the mess we were behind closed doors.

I was still fuming hours later when the house grew completely quiet. I'd heard Sebastian go to bed and even though I was tired from too many late nights out with Adam, I left the house, this time with Harry at my side.

Even though I was always excited to see Adam, tonight felt different. I'd let Georgina and her bull crap ruin my mood, so when I got to the field and Adam was already there sitting in the grass, I didn't greet him like I usually did. Harry did, however. He and Adam had become fast friends. I watched him try to sit his big body in Adam's lap while I lay out the blanket and I was only a little jealous.

I plopped down and lay back hard, a long sigh leaving me. I was glad to be out of that house, but I was still more than a little pissed off.

Adam sat next to me and Harry settled in next to him. I gave Harry a look that said traitor.

"What's up?" Adam questioned, looking down at me.

I shrugged as best as I could lying on the ground. "Same ole, same ole."

"Bullshit, Livvy. What's going on?"

I almost smiled. He called me Livvy. And no one had ever called me that. It was sweet. So sweet, I almost wished I could taste that moment and not just feel it.

I shook my head like I wasn't going to answer, but I did, because it was Adam and I was me. And I couldn't refuse him even if I didn't want to talk about it all. "Just my stepmonster."

"Your stepmonster?"

We hadn't talked about my parents since that night I'd yelled at him that I came out here to talk to my parents since they were dead. He seemed to get that I would tell him more when I was ready to, so he hadn't pressed. I appreciated that about Adam. He wasn't nosey or impatient. No, he'd wait. He was like a rock.

"Yeah, I have a really crazy town, snobby stepmonster and a creepy stepbrother that I am pretty sure wants to knock the boots with me."

His body locked tight next to mine and the coldness swept into his eyes like a blizzard hitting the north. "What did you say?"

"I said, I have a really crazy town step—"

He held up a hand. "Skip that part and go right to your creepy stepbrother."

I shrugged again. "I think he wants to sleep with me. He's creepy and inappropriate."

Anger blanketed his face. And Adam mad was a scary thing. "Has he touched you?"

I shook my head. "No, he's careful of that. He just comes on too strong and says things."

I looked away because it embarrassed me. I'd never told anyone and it never happened when my dad was alive. I didn't know if he was intimidated, but as soon as he was gone, Sebastian started up his antics. We were never really close, but now I hated him.

"Like what things?" he ground out from above me. He was getting scarier by the second in his anger, but I only smiled. I knew in my heart this boy would never hurt me. The butterflies in my stomach told their own story. They loved how he was protective of me.

"Just stupid shit. I don't think he'd ever actually do anything. He knows I've never even kissed a boy. The boys at school stay far away from me." I got embarrassed at all the information I'd just divulged. "I don't want to talk about it."

He got up off the blanket in record time and reached into his pocket, pulling out his pack of cigarettes and a lighter. He paced the spot in front of me, back and forth, lighting up. He took a couple of drags before he stopped and pressed the heels of both of his hands to his eyes, his cigarette dangling from his right hand.

"Fuck. This is why you don't want to go home. This is why you hang out here."

I gave him a sad smile. "Not totally. My dad brought me here before he died. It was where he said goodbye." I felt a burn in my nose that told me tears weren't far behind it, so I looked away from him and stared at the bridge in the distance.

I felt him sit down near my feet and I smelled the scent of smoke, but it smelled good. Sweet and spicy all at once. I peered at him from beneath heavy lids and noticed the cigarettes were brown.

"What are you smoking?"

He took it out of his mouth and gave it a look while blowing out smoke rings. I'd never been a girl attracted to bad boys. I liked nice guys. Kind people. And maybe Adam was all of those things, too, but in that moment, he looked so very, very bad. With his disheveled dark hair and tattoos, sitting with his legs up, his elbows resting on his knees, a sweet, delicious cigarette dangling from his mouth. It did things to me I wasn't ready to admit I was ready for yet. My nipples pebbled beneath my bra. The place between my legs ached.

"Cloves."

"Mmmm. They smell good," I breathed and God, I sounded sexy, my voice husky and Adam just looked on. His eyes roamed over me over and over again. He liked to watch me, I remembered, and so I let him until he eventually got up and paced again. I smiled, knowing he was uncomfortable. Some people might not be able to read Adam Nova, but I was not one of those people. I'd known him for weeks and I knew the more he pulled away, the more uncomfortable he was.

He stomped out his cigarette and I shot him a look, so he picked it up off the ground and shoved it in his pocket before sitting right next to me on the blanket and lying back, his head next to mine.

"Tell me about your dad."

And I wanted to. I wanted to tell him everything in that moment. But he'd held too many things back from me. He was still hiding and I wanted to know more about him. It seemed like all we did out here most of the time was talk about me and my days and problems and loves and likes and hates.

So, I picked a subject I thought might be easy to discuss. "Tell me about your tattoos first."

I was looking at the sky, but I could feel him staring at my face from beside me. There was no answer and silence for what felt like forever but was probably only just a minute in time before he spoke.

"I like them."

I smiled and met his eyes with my own this time. My eyes trailed down to the tiger right over his Adam's apple. "I figured as much, Nova. How about you tell me why you like them."

He sucked on his bottom lip and seemed to stare past me for a second before answering. "They make me feel safe."

Instinctively I moved my hand between us closer to his, until the back of it brushed the back of his hand. I wanted to wrap my fingers around his. He seemed so vulnerable in that moment and I knew how hard that must have been for him. I wanted to wrap my arms around him. *I* wanted to make him feel safe.

I wanted to ask him why they made him feel safe, but I had a feeling that may have been pushing his limits when he'd already shared something so personal.

In an effort to lighten the conversation and I'm not gonna lie, it was an opportunity to touch him and I hardly ever did that, I ran my finger down the back of his hand between us where I knew the face of a wolf was tattooed. "And what about him? Who's he?" I grinned at him.

He didn't smile back, but his eyes did. "That's Lupus."

I couldn't help my smile. "Lupus, huh?"

"Yep, Greek for wolf and he is one of the eighty-eight constellations in modern astronomy."

Who was this guy? The things he knew. The stuff he said. He was one big contradiction I couldn't get enough of. His tattoos and attitude screamed bad boy, but his mind? It screamed nerd. I loved it.

I nodded to the tiger on his neck. "And that guy?"

He rubbed his hand over the tiger before answering. "That's the White Tiger of the West. It's a Chinese constellation and it represents the west and the autumn season."

I gestured toward his body. "Are they all constellations?"

"Not all. Some are stars. Some planets. Galaxies."

"Who does them?" I felt like we were on a roll now. He was opening up. His eyes were lit up like a kid at Christmas. His deep blues were filled with passion.

"My best friend, Raven, works at Slinging Ink, downtown."

I looked over his ink one more time before responding. "He's really talented."

He gave me a funny look before nodding and saying, "Yep."

"And how did you learn so much about the stars?"

A wall shot down between us like a door closing with a bang. The passion faded. The connection broke and we were back at square one. I was surprised he didn't jump up to smoke and pace again. No, he just turned away, his expression shuttered. He was a locked door, but at least he answered me.

"My mom," he said softly and gruff. Like it hurt to say. "She was an astronomer. Not a real one, but an amateur. She studied the stars and planets for fun."

My heart went out to him. *She was. She studied.* All past tense. He'd lost people he loved, too. God, I wanted to hold him. But I was too scared he'd push me away forever. And I wasn't ready for whatever this was to be over yet.

"And she taught you?"

He let out a pained breath before answering. "Yeah, I guess she did." He said it into the sky like he couldn't even bear to look at me. He was hiding. Always hiding, and I wondered if maybe that was why his tattoos made him feel safe.

His eyes whipped to mine. "Now, tell me about your dad."

And so I did. I told him about how my mom died at childbirth, but my dad never blamed me. He loved me, despite what me being here caused him to lose. I told him how he was a struggling artist, a painter. And how we'd been poor most of my life until one day, he'd been discovered. And like a whirlwind, we went from rags to riches. It seemed surreal now. I told him how he'd been sick for years before he passed, but that he was a good father and that I missed him every day.

And in the midst of all of that, I felt the back of Adam's hand move against mine until our hands overlapped and his fingers steepled mine. He brushed them slowly, his fingers feeling all of the wrinkles of mine before fully grasping my hand. I imagined that's how he did most things, with so much thought, methodically, slow, sweet. And when he finally cradled my hand in his, it happened. My heart, it got hot and big in my chest and that heat, it spread outward, burning my entire body, making me feel warm all over. A fever it felt like. It was the very first time for me. The hand-holding. This heat. And all from a simple handhold. It was the first time my heart ever caught a fever, but it wouldn't be the last. Not as long as Adam was around.

CHAPTER 11

Liv

I stared at the empty field in front of me like it was a foreign place and I guess in a way it was. It had been so, so long since I'd shown up here and been alone. I'd been sneaking away to be close to Adam for a month unbeknownst to anyone but us. And he'd always been here, waiting on me. Except for the last three days and they'd been a helluva three days. I felt like I was going stir-crazy without him.

It was day three and still no Adam. I felt my panic ratchet up a notch. Maybe this was it. I'd felt it for weeks now. As I pushed closer to him, he pulled away. Almost like I scared him. Almost like maybe he'd only wanted friendship from me. How many times in the last month had I begged him with my eyes and heart to kiss me? Hold me?

He'd never taken it further than the hand-holding and that had been momentous in itself. But God, I wanted more. I wanted all of him. I wanted all the teenage fantasies that had seemed so stupid only weeks ago.

I wanted Adam Nova to be my boyfriend, damn it.

I looked around the field again for maybe a message in a bottle or some kind of indication that he had been here. I'd done this every day for the last three days and on my walk here today I knew. I knew he wasn't going to be here, so I wasn't surprised, just mostly disappointed as hell. I'd basically been a space cadet the last few days, worried about him. Worried about us.

I stood there, kicking myself in the ass for not exchanging phone numbers with him just like I had yesterday and the day before. For not demanding that he give me a way to contact him. But it had seemed so romantic. Us meeting in this field under the stars and sometimes lying there and talking for hours. Well, mostly me talking. Adam was still a closed book most days. But sometimes he'd crack open and show me a page and those days felt like rare, precious gems. Yes, those days. Those intimate moments I stored in the center of my heart. Our nights together were sweet. Sometimes we just looked at the sky silently. I realized what a mistake this was now, because I had no way to contact him. No way to know if he was okay. No way to know if he was ghosting my ass.

I didn't even know where he lived. I paced my spot in the field, chewing on my fingernail, thinking that maybe I should have brought Harry. What if someone came up on me and since Adam wasn't here, I was alone?

I thought of all the things Adam had told me while we lay in this spot and realized he hadn't told me much at all. Except the fact his best friend, Raven, did his tattoos and that he worked at Slinging Ink.

I could go there and ask Raven if he'd seen him. God, I sounded pathetic. But I was genuinely worried. I knew in my heart that if Adam couldn't make it, he would try to contact me. Also, if he was trying to get rid of me, I thought that maybe he should show the common courtesy of freaking letting me know, to my face.

I pulled my phone out of my pocket and started the maps app, typing in the tattoo parlor as I started walking toward North Madison.

It was only a fifteen-minute walk. I could do that. I was a brave, bad chick. I was only five minutes into my walk when I realized this might have been a huge mistake. It was dark and the streets were poorly lit and I'd seen more homeless people in the last five minutes than I'd collectively ever seen in my life. I'd been asked for a cigarette, money, and food. And I was pretty sure I'd seen a hooker if her attire was any indication.

By the time I'd made it to Slinging Ink, I was such a bundle of nerves that the jingle of a bell when I opened the door almost made me jump out of my skin. I looked up from nearly falling over the threshold of the doorway to find what looked like a boy covered in tattoos and too many piercings in his face to count, sitting behind the wooden counter, smiling. He only looked a couple of years older than me and even though he was covered in art and hardware, he was devastatingly pretty with short styled blond hair and sparkling blue eyes that seemed to be dancing with humor. He seemed to enjoy watching me almost bust my behind.

I pulled the bottom of my shirt a bit, trying to right it because I felt so out of place and nervous to boot.

I cleared my throat awkwardly as I approached the desk, but before I could say anything, the boy at the front desk spoke.

"And how can I help you, baby?"

And if I thought I was nervous before—wrong! I opened mouth and closed it about five thousand times because what did one say when she was trying to hunt down the boy she really liked to one of the most beautiful men she'd ever seen?

His eyes roved over my entire body, making me feel hot and twitchy. I rocked back and forth on my toes and swallowed.

"You here for a tattoo?" He smiled wickedly before pulling the ring in his lip into his mouth and giving it a good suck. "I can do you."

Oh, I bet he could.

I fanned my face with my right hand and smiled awkwardly.

"I'm looking for Raven?"

At that, his smile fell and he rolled the ring in his lip with his tongue before muttering, "Of course you are." He shook his head. "That bitch has all the luck."

And then he was gone in a flash behind a black partition that separated the waiting area from the rest of the parlor.

I waited for what seemed like forever, but the time on my phone said it was only fifteen minutes before a stunning dark-haired woman appeared behind the counter.

Her beautifully pale arms were covered in colorful floral tattoos that went all the way up and underneath her sleeves. Her dark hair was cut in a stylish pixie cut that was full-on shaved on one side. The other side of her hair hung low over one of her hazel green eyes. Her face was narrow with high cheekbones and she had some of the most plump and inviting lips I'd ever seen, even if they were covered in black lipstick.

She wore a black T-shirt with a big star in the middle with the words Madison Planetarium over it.

She smiled at me as I stared her down. "Can I help you?"

"Oh. Oh. Uhm." I looked behind her, expecting Raven to pop out from behind that partition any moment. "I'm looking for Raven."

Her smile grew and this time she showed me her straight pearly whites. Her hand shot out across the desk. "I'm Raven."

I felt my mouth fall open, but my Southern manners didn't fail me as my own hand made its way across the desk and into hers, giving it a squeeze.

I let go of her hand and stepped back, not knowing what the hell to say.

Raven, Adam's best friend and tattoo artist, was a girl. A really freaking pretty girl. She wasn't a boney, not quite grown into her body teenage girl. No, she was more woman, with curves, and grace, and my God, she knew how to do eyeliner like a damn pro. I didn't even wear lipstick or mascara. I wanted to die.

"What can I do for you?"

She was still smiling and looking like some guy's gothic dream. And I had no clue what to say, so I just muddled through the truth.

"I'm looking for a friend."

Her eyebrows shot up. "Are you now?" She winked and I felt my face flush.

I cleared my throat. "Adam. Do you know Adam Nova?"

Her eyes lit with recognition and I was relieved and pissed and thinking that this was basically the dumbest thing I'd ever done in my life.

Her eyes took me in from the top of my head to the tips of my toes slowly before asking, "You're looking for Adam?"

She said "You're" like it was the most unbelievable thing in the world. And I guess looking me over, she could see I wasn't from around here. That I was out of place. That Adam and I were completely different.

"Yeah. Uhm. We've had an appointment every weekday for the past month, but I haven't heard from him in three days." An appointment? What the hell was wrong with me? I picked at the bottom of my shirt. "I'm worried."

God, this gorgeous woman probably thought I was stalking her boyfriend. I was an idiot, teenage girl and I'd let a man play me. With the stars, for fuck's sake. I needed to get the hell out of there before I made more of a fool of myself.

"You know what?" I turned to walk out the door. "Never mind. This was a mistake."

Raven flew around the counter and was standing in front of the door I was about to walk out of in a few seconds' time. She held her hand up. "No, wait." Seriousness painted her features. "Just hold on. I'll give him a call."

Digging a cell phone from her jeans pocket, she gave me a small smile and then went back around the wooden desk, taking a seat on a stool and throwing her feet up on the desk. She gave me another wink and I blushed down to my bones.

"Heyyy, Nova." She said his name like she'd said it a thousand times in a thousand different ways and I felt my embarrassed flush become one of anger, but I listened on, unable not to, but afraid he would tell her to send me home. That he was done with me.

"You've been keeping secrets from me, asshole," she said in a sing-song voice, her eyes never leaving mine.

She listened intently, her eyebrows raised, like she found this whole thing very intriguing. "I have a friend of yours here looking for you." There was a pause. "Mmmhmm." It was a purr, deliberately sexy and cute all at once. Then with twinkling eyes, she asked, "What's your name, pretty girl?"

"Liv," I whispered, but she must have been paying extra close attention because she had no trouble relaying my name back to Adam.

"Well then, you better hurry. Ry had his eye on her and me, well, both of my eyes are on her," she finished with a laugh and hung up.

She stared at me, her smile gone, her face questioning. She looked at me like I was a puzzle she was trying to put together.

With analyzing eyes, she finally said, "He's on his way. He said to wait here."

A moment of panic hit me like a freight train. What in the hell was I doing here? He was going to be so pissed that I'd hunted him down. She'd found him easily, so surely if he'd wanted to come see me, he would have. Would she be pissed at him once he got here? This was a huge mistake and I was already feeling embarrassed about it.

Raven must have seen the dread on my face because she stood up and walked into the waiting room and stood in front of the door as she said, "Uh uh uh, gorgeous. He said you weren't to leave."

And even though I'd never even been kissed, never been touched sexually, I knew in that moment I was somehow truly fucked.

CHAPTER 12

Adam

I was going to kill Livingston Montgomery. Right after I
made sure she was alive and unharmed. Those were
my thoughts as I raced through the streets of North
Madison. What in the hell was she thinking coming
out here all by herself? There were a lot of things about
Liv I didn't know still, but I definitely knew she was
smart. A hell of a lot smarter than she was being right
now.

I was pissed. So damn angry at her. I hadn't planned
on leaving my dad. He needed me right now, but Liv
had made the decision for me when she'd come looking for me. I'd wanted to get down to the field and at
least leave a message for her, but I hadn't been able to. I
hadn't even made it to school or work in the past three
days.

My heart pounded as I walked through the streets
seeing it all through her eyes. The neighborhood was
littered with the impoverished, starved, and homeless.
The hookers, the trash. It was a different world over

on the mainland. One I was sure she'd never witnessed before. She must have been terrified and by the time I made it to the tattoo shop, my anger had taken a back seat to worry.

I flew through the doors, almost knocking Raven on her ass as I plowed through the entryway, familiar bells tinkling above my head. And there she was, standing in the corner near an old plant, looking terrified and so goddamn beautiful I couldn't catch my breath. She was wearing the white dress with the thin straps that I loved and I didn't know if I should kiss her or spank her. God, I'd missed her. I hadn't stopped thinking about her the last three days.

She looked odd there in that tattoo parlor. Because it was my world. I'd only ever seen her on the island or in that field. It was almost like I made her up, but seeing her there in that shady tattoo parlor on my side of town put things into perspective I'd never wanted to consider. The biggest thing being that Livingston Montgomery didn't belong here. No, she belonged on the beach in her mansion, driving expensive cars and wearing pricey things. The good life.

The reality of that all burned as I raced toward her and pulled her into my arms. God, she was a sight for sore eyes. I'd never hugged Liv and as I wrapped my arms around her and held her close to my chest, I realized I'd been missing out on a fuck of a lot of goodness.

I held her tight, thankful that she was okay, and in that moment, I was acutely aware of how much I'd missed her the last three days and that scared the shit out of me.

I pulled out of our hug and held her at arm's length, my hands at the tops of her shoulders. "What the hell were you thinking coming here?"

She'd been smiling not two seconds before, now not so much. Her face fell, at first sad and then her entire body locked tight and her eyes ignited with anger.

"What the hell are you thinking talking to me like that?" She backed out of my embrace and shrugged my hands off.

Raven laughed and I glared at her over my shoulder.

"Oh, don't give me that look. You have some splain'in to do, Lucy. You've been hiding pretty girls from me." She gave Liv a once-over that made me prickly as hell before turning her eyes back to me. She squinted her eyes, studying me with the kind of inquisitiveness that made me nervous. "Why?" she asked in all seriousness.

But I couldn't think about anything except for getting Liv out of there and back where she belonged—on the island.

"Later," I ground out as I grabbed Liv's hand and pulled her through the door and out onto the street. She was practically running behind me when we came up on the next block.

"Let me go, you freaking brute!" she yelled as she tried to pull her hand from mine.

"No." I clutched her hand more firmly while we paused at a road where cars were crossing.

"No? Where are you pulling me to?" She tried wrenching her hand free once again, but I held fast. "An hour ago, you'd stood me up for the third day in a row and now you won't let me go?"

"I didn't fucking stand you up." I gave her a sharp look. "We didn't have a standing date, Liv, and I had shit to do."

"Great, well, let me go. Now, I have shit to do, too."

Her attitude only made my anger worse. The girl didn't care about her safety. It was clear from the moment she'd come back to the field after Boone had put his hands on her. It was even clearer now. How could she risk herself by coming here to look for me this time of night?

I stopped on the sidewalk, turning on her until we were nose to nose. "What the fuck were you thinking coming out here alone? Do you not realize how dumb that is?"

Her teeth clacked together in anger. "Call me dumb one more time, Nova! I. Dare. You!" she shouted into my face.

Grabbing her hand, I pulled her down the street again, this time at warp speed, my chest heaving in exasperation.

"Where are you taking me?" she shouted from behind me.

"Home," I threw over my shoulder as I felt a fat raindrop land on my cheek. Great! Just what I needed, a damn thunderstorm in the middle of the freaking shit storm that was my life right now.

She yanked hard, her hand slipping from mine. "I don't need you to walk me home, Adam. I know how to get there all on my own." She turned down a dark alley that cut through two old brick buildings. I let out a long sigh, praying for patience as I jogged to catch up with her. There was no way in hell she was walking this neighborhood by herself again. I wanted to scream.

"You can't walk home alone, Liv. It's not safe out here. You shouldn't have come, especially after dark."

"Go away, Adam!" Her voice echoed off the two buildings surrounding us.

"Why?" I yelled it. She was being irrational and acting like a maniac and I couldn't figure out what the hell she wanted me to do.

She paused in front of me and I saw one, two, three raindrops hit her bare shoulders. "Why?" Her look was incredulous. "We're doing this then? If we're asking why, then I have a lot of fucking questions."

I flinched at the word fucking. I hardly ever heard Liv cuss and the sound offended my ears. She was too good for those kinds of words. Too sweet, too perfect.

"Like why haven't you come to see me in three days?" She held up a hand, ticking off a finger and the next. "Why don't you ever tell me anything? And most of all…" She paused and it felt like it was for dramatic effect, so I shut my mouth like any smart man. "Why didn't you tell me Raven was a fucking girl?"

I held my finger up to her face. "Stop fucking cussing," I gritted out. Jesus, I was a contradictory asshole, but this was exactly what Liv did to me. She made me insane.

She let out a sarcastic laugh as she tilted her head

to the sky and when she did, it was like she was calling to the rain gods themselves because the sky opened up and huge raindrops pummeled us.

I grabbed her hand and raced for a small overhang in the alley that didn't really do shit to cover us. I pressed her into the wall with my front, trying to keep her dry, but it was almost useless. We were soaking wet and only getting wetter by the second.

She looked up at me from behind thick, dripping eyelashes. "Why didn't you tell me Raven was a girl? Is she your girlfriend? Why did you lie to me?"

Jesus, was that what she thought? This girl was out of her mind. I hadn't been able to think about anyone but her since I'd seen her the first time. Didn't she understand? Couldn't she see it?

"I didn't lie to you. I just didn't correct you when you thought she was a dude." I pushed the wet hair off my forehead with my hands and stared down at her, softening my voice. "I didn't think it was important. And she never came up again. I just forgot about it."

She curled her lip. "You forgot? How convenient. Did you also forget to meet me these last three days?"

I muscled my way into her body, until my legs were between hers, my torso pressed into her big breasts that I hadn't been able to get my dirty mind off for over a month.

Fuck, it felt good there. Right at home, pressed up against her like this, so I stupidly leaned forward and buried my face right in her neck, enjoying the scent of the rain and my Luna.

Taking a deep breath, I lifted my head and brought my forehead to the wall right beside her head and my lips to her ear. "You know better, Livvy. I could never forget about you. Not yesterday. Not today. Not tomorrow. Not ever." It was too true. I'd tried for weeks to get this girl out of my head, all to no avail.

A shiver went through her at my whisper and her tense body melted into mine like butter. And while the rain pounded down on us, she wrapped her arms around my neck and buried her face in my soaking wet shirt, and that's when I realized that while hugging Liv had been one of the best things ever, it in no way compared to Liv hugging me.

I soaked up that hug like I was standing in the sunshine instead of the downpour of a cold rain. I couldn't help it. I brought my hands up and cradled the sides of her small, heart-shaped face and used my thumbs to tilt her chin so I could see her eyes.

Baby browns framed in the thickest lashes I'd ever seen stared up at me with such emotion, such feeling that I knew I was done. This girl who was too good for me. Too sweet. Too fucking amazing and she was going to end me. And I was starting to be totally okay with that. What I wasn't okay with was ruining her.

"Why do you hide from me, Adam Nova?" she said softly, her eyes searching mine for answers I couldn't give.

I couldn't answer. I didn't know how, so instead I laid my forehead to hers, our lips only a breath apart, my heart beating a million miles a minute. Because I knew what was coming. I was looking forward to it. I was terrified of it.

Her brown hair plastered to her head, her white dress soaked through, her hand on my cheek now, she asked, "Why won't you let me in?"

Jesus, she wanted in. I wanted her in, too. But I didn't know how to let people in. Since I'd lost my mother, I'd kept people at arm's length. And I couldn't let Liv in. Not Liv with her dreamy looks and unfailing optimism even though she'd lost her mother, and then her father. How could I let her in when she was pure light and I was nothing but darkness?

"I don't know how," I barely choked out, for the first time since I could remember baring myself, my heart.

Sadness radiated from her eyes as she stood on tip-toe, her face ominously close to mine, and I felt my eyes flutter closed at the prospect of what I knew was coming. Because even though I'd fought it for weeks, I wanted it more than I wanted anything.

Her breath ghosted across my mouth. "I'll teach you," she murmured against my lips and I felt the brush of her lips against mine all the way to my toes.

And then her lips were on mine, lightly pecking my bottom lip and then sucking the middle of my top. I let out a groan. I couldn't believe it. This girl. I wouldn't kiss her, so she said fuck it and kissed me.

She was fearless and brazen and wonderful. And she was mine if I wanted her. I didn't deserve her.

Those small kisses were unexpected and shocking and amazing and before I knew what I was doing I'd pushed in closer if possible and taken her mouth, biting her pillowy bottom lip. Slipping my tongue into her mouth savagely. I'd dreamed of tasting her for too long and now I was like an animal on its prey, blinded by pure hunger and time.

I should have been thinking about how this was her first kiss, but the truth of it was, it felt like it was mine, too, so I was selfish. The first slide of her tongue against mine, the first nibble of her teeth, the first suck of her lips. It was unlike any kiss I'd ever experienced and I was transported back to the field and under the stars. Comets tore across the sky, meteors pummeled the Earth, asteroids exploded.

Forget setting the world on fire. Liv and I? We were going to burn down the universe.

My hands were in her hair.

My mouth crushed to hers.

My feet firmly to the pavement.

But my mind, it was gone.

There wasn't rationale in kisses like this.

No, these kisses were unhinged passion, insanity—mad.

"Mmm," she moaned into my mouth and I siphoned it down, taking it all. I wanted everything from her. I wanted my mouth on every inch of her body. So, I took and I moved my mouth down her neck to the hollow spot at the base of her throat, licking and then sucking.

But God, all I could think of was the other places I wanted to taste her. The sunken spot at the top of her shoulder. The tops of her breasts. The tips of them.

The divot of her belly button. The soft spot behind her knees. The swell of her ankle. The wetness between her legs.

I was drunk, dizzy on my thoughts and her moans when I heard a sound nearby that had me jerking back and looking around the dark, rainy alley, until I finally looked back at her. She smiled.

"Probably a cat." Her innocent, round eyes looked up at me.

I looked down at her and smiled, too. "Maybe. But I need to get you out of the rain and somewhere safe." I grabbed her hand to pull her again, but she wasn't having it.

"No way. You have some questions to answer before I go anywhere with you, Nova."

Christ, this crazy girl was going to make me answer all of her questions in the fucking rain in the middle of the night. I wanted to bang my head on the wall behind her.

"But we kissed. Everything's great." I was talking out of my ass and trying to get her to let this go long enough for us to get somewhere safe and dry.

"Wrong. I kissed you." She batted her eyelashes. "And I'm calling the shots."

"Fine, hurry up. It's fucking pouring." I pushed the wet hair off my forehead.

"Is Raven your girlfriend?"

Horrified, I answered, "What? Absolutely not."

Her eyes narrowed. "Has she ever been your girlfriend?"

Lord. I couldn't do anything but laugh at the pure ridiculousness of this situation. "Jesus, you're being insane. Let's just get out of the rain and I'll tell you everything."

"No." Her face spoke volumes about her resolve, so I just answered the question.

"Raven has never been my girlfriend."

"Have you ever had sex with her?"

"Never."

"Have you ever kissed her?"

I pinched the bridge of my nose, feeling positively fucking violent.

"No."

Confusion filled her face. "Hmm?"

"Oh, for fuck's sake, what now?" The rain was a steady stream and the overhang was barely sheltering us.

"I don't understand why."

"Why what?" I almost yelled.

"Why you haven't kissed her or tried something with her. She's gorgeous and seems like your type."

Why couldn't she see it? Her crazy, stargazing, having conversations in the pouring rain ass was my type. So, I leaned forward and grabbed her chin with my fingers.

"I haven't been with Raven because she's definitely not my type, Liv. No, my type is a pain in the ass from the island who wants to have hour-long confrontations in the rain and loves the stars. That's my type, baby. Okay?"

She nodded, starry-eyed. "Okay," she murmured.

Thankful I'd finally gotten through to her, I let go of her face and backed away. "Also, I haven't been with Raven because she's a lesbian and we've never been interested in each other way."

She sucked in a gasp as surprise painted her features. "Ohhh."

I nodded.

Her brow furrowed and she slipped her hand into mine before pulling me down the alley and through the rain. "Well, you should have started with that, Nova. It's freaking freezing and we've been out here having a chat in the rain like two crazy people." She looked affronted. "I could have caught pneumonia."

I couldn't help it. I threw my head back and laughed. The sound of it echoed around us and we clung to each other in a dark, dirty alley. I looked down at her, my cheeks burning from the laughter. She smiled up at me and I realized, I was happy. For the first time in years this girl had made me smile and laugh and truly be happy. It was a bittersweet moment, there in the dark, feeling like a ray of light was somehow peeking through. Because I knew what kind of costs came with happiness. I knew it was temporary. And I knew it was fleeting. And I told myself all I could do was enjoy it while it lasted.

CHAPTER 13

Liv

I was walking in the dark streets with Adam, but I wasn't seeing a gosh darn thing, because my hand was in his now like it belonged there, for heaven's sake. It was big and warm and I thought my heart might burst right open. And he'd kissed me. I'd been kissed. Not just some little, small kiss either. Sure, I'd taken the first step and laid one on him, but I'd felt like it was time and I was done waiting. But I hadn't expected that. Not the slip of his tongue or the sting of his teeth. I didn't expect a full-on mouth invasion. And I didn't think that first kisses were supposed to be like the one Adam gave me. Because it wasn't a fumbling, messy, awkward kiss. No, it was a kiss to end all kisses. A kiss that would put every future kisses I ever had to shame. And his taste. He had tasted like sweet smoke and mint and pure manly goodness. I couldn't stop thinking about it. Obsessing over it. And even though it had only been ten minutes, I knew I'd still be thinking about it in ten years, too. It was a kiss to remember. Yeah, the heart fever was back in full effect.

I was walking around in a kiss stupor when I realized we weren't headed back to the field or the island. We were walking down a long road of old apartment buildings, the rain at a steady drizzle now. "Where are we going?"

I sounded like I was still in a daze and I touched my lips realizing they still felt swollen and hot. All I could think of was how I wanted more kisses from Adam. Right now. All the time. Anywhere. Everywhere.

"Home."

I pulled my hand from his. "But my home isn't this way."

"Nope, but mine is."

"Oh." That was all I could say. He was taking me to his home. What in the hell was happening? I felt like I was dreaming. He was kissing me. And holding my hand and now he was taking me home. I wondered if I was going to get to meet his family. I was damn near giddy.

We walked through the bad part of town and eventually hit a dilapidated apartment building and while I knew Adam didn't have much, it finally occurred to me exactly how poor he was.

My father and I had been lower middle class before he'd made it. And as we walked through the halls and up the stairs of the apartment building, I realized we had never been as poor as Adam and his family. No, this was definitely lower class. Our wet shoes squeaked against the floors and there was the faint scent of mold in the air.

A female voice called out behind us, "Where you going, baby?"

And I turned to find what looked like a strung-out girl not much older than me coming out of her apartment door.

Adam spared her a small glance before saying, "Go back to bed, Mona."

Her glazed over eyes took me in and she smiled. "Who you got with you?"

"None of your business."

I followed Adam up the stairs as we left Mona behind. I felt bad for her.

"That was sad," I mumbled, following Adam up.

He shrugged his shoulders. "This whole damn place is sad, Liv. Why do you think I meet you in the field?"

He wasn't hiding me? Or ghosting me? He was protecting me from this part of his life and that made me a whole new kind of sad. This time for Adam.

With the jingle of his keys, he opened the door to his apartment and we walked in to a brown, threadbare carpet and a not much better brown sofa, but the place looked and smelled clean. It was an open floor plan with a decent size living room attached to a small dining area off to the side and a small kitchen in the corner. On each end of the room were two doorways I assumed led to bedrooms.

And then it occurred to me. What if Adam lived here alone? I'd never asked his age. Oh my God, what if he just looked young and was like twenty-three? Holy shit, that was definitely not going to fly with the stepmonster. The tattoos and smoking would probably be enough to send her over the edge, anyway.

"How old are you?"

He smiled. "Now she asks."

My chest tightened in panic because he looked way too smug. "Oh my God, you're like thirty, aren't you? Oh my God!" I started to pace the room.

Adam's eyes rolled and his head shook back and forth slowly. "Chill out, crazy lady. I'm only nineteen."

Whew. I almost had a freaking heart attack.

"Hold on one second," he said, pulling off his wet T-shirt, and I thought my eyes were going to cross. Because damn, he looked good. I mean, he looked good clothed, but he looked even better not. "I need to check on my dad."

Oh, so his dad *was* here.

"*Hijo*, is that you? Who's there with you?"

Adam gave me an almost smile. "Yeah, Dad, it's me. I have a friend with me."

"A female friend, maybe? Do I hear a girl, *hijo*?"

A full-blown smile now covered Adam's lips as he rolled his eyes at his father, but I barely noticed, because nipples and abs and dear Lord those pants were low. God, his skin was a light brown and his torso was long and sinewy. I wanted to stare. A lot. So it was only a little awkward when I stared and looked away and then stared and looked away again. I was hoping he wouldn't notice, but if the heat in his eyes was anything to go by, he totally did. And his heat made me hot all over. Lord help me.

"I'm coming, Pops. Give me a second."

Adam threw his shirt on the kitchen counter and turned toward a dark room off the main area.

"Bring your friend, too, Adam. I want to see her."

Adam looked back at me clearly embarrassed before gesturing for me to follow him. I pulled on the bottom of my wet dress and smoothed my hair back. I would meet Adam's dad looking like a drowned rat. Great.

He turned the light on as we entered a small bedroom with the same brown carpet. It was sparsely decorated. Only a photograph of the stars over a queen bed. A solitary dresser was pushed against the wall opposite. Nothing else occupied the room besides a small end table that sat next to the bed. And in the middle of the bed sat a big Hispanic man. A very good-looking middle-aged Hispanic man.

He had gauze on his forehead and a huge smile on his face at the sight of me.

Adam walked to the bed while I stood in the doorway, trying to be invisible. I was a nervous wreck. I'd never met the parents.

"How you doing, Pops? Any pain? Hungry?" Adam tried pulling his covers up around him and the big man sat up further and shooed Adam's hands away.

"Move, son, move. I'm trying to meet your friend. Come closer, *nena linda*." He waved me over and as Adam backed away with a grin, I moved forward.

He studied me as I studied him. His eyes were a

deep chocolatey brown and even though his hair was too long and wrinkles bracketed the corners of his kind eyes, I imagined this man was beautiful in his youth because he definitely wasn't bad to look at now. "My son has good taste, yes?" he said, his eyes dancing with humor and flirtation.

I couldn't help but smile back at him even as I blushed down to my very bones.

"What's your name, *niña*?"

"Livingston."

He was too quick with an answer to not know it already. "Beautiful name for a beautiful girl. I can see why my son hasn't been home lately." He shot Adam a knowing look before gazing back at me. "I'm José. It's very nice to meet you, Livingston. Do you work? Go to school? Where do you live? How old are you?"

"Okay, okay, Pops! That's enough of an interrogation tonight. You're supposed to be resting and I need to get Liv a change of clothes. She's soaking wet from the rain."

"Fine, but you must bring her back when I'm feeling better. I'll make Mom's pastélon and she can tell me everything."

Adam poured some water from a pitcher on the dresser into a cup and set it on a small table next to the bed and made sure the covers were straight around his dad. "I can hardly wait," he mumbled.

Longing blasted through me. Seeing Adam with his obviously kind father made me miss my own.

Adam snapped off the light on his way out as his

father said, "It was nice meeting you, Livingston."

I smiled at José, already deciding he was pretty awesome. "Nice meeting you, too, Mr. Nova."

He shook his head and laid his hand over his heart. "You wound me, *niña*! I am no old man. Mr. Nova is my father. You call me José, yes?"

I giggled. "Okay, José."

"Perfecto." His eyes moved to Adam. "Goodnight, *hijo. Te amo.*"

We headed out of the room as Adam said, "I love you, too, Pops."

As I followed Adam across the living area I couldn't help but think of how lucky he was to have such a loving father. He was a character for sure, but I was willing to bet they had a lot of fun together. I was willing to wager that the gauze on his father's forehead was the reason I hadn't seen him for days.

"You've been taking care of your dad." I was stating the obvious. And as we entered Adam's room he gave me an explanation that made me feel like absolute crap for thinking he was ghosting me.

"Yeah, he fell down the stairs a few days ago and hit his head. The damn elevators were broken. Stupid piece of shit building. He likes to go down there and play cards with his friends. He has a bad leg and has no damn business taking the stairs, but I was at school. Mona found him and called the ambulance. They kept him a few days and I couldn't leave him." His soft eyes told me he thought of me while he was taking care of his dad. That he wished he could have let me know what was going on.

"I'm sorry. I'm glad he's home and okay."

He inclined his head. "Yeah, me, too."

"And I also think we should exchange phone numbers so that never happens again." I laughed.

"What? You didn't like meeting Raven and having our first argument in a dark alley while it's pouring rain?"

The fact he said our first argument made me feel good. Like maybe there actually was an us and that we'd be around long enough to argue again. There wasn't anyone else on earth I wanted to argue with besides Adam. Especially if all of the arguments ended with *the kiss. The fever.*

Adam's room wasn't much different than his dad's. It was minimally decorated and as soon as we entered, Adam started stripping what was left of his clothes off. I turned around to give him some privacy and I heard him snicker. My face burned. I wanted to watch him take his wet pants off. I really did, but I thought I'd probably had all I could handle tonight with that kiss and those abs.

My heart pounded in my chest as I heard the rustling of clothes. Finally, Adam appeared in front of me in nothing but low-slung track pants, holding out a black T-shirt and a pair of black gym shorts. I stared because, oh my God, I'd fantasized a lot about this boy in the past couple of weeks. Hell, I'd fantasized about him before I even met him, but nothing compared to the real thing and it was pretty spectacular. Those dark brown nipples were calling my name. I wanted to touch them, taste them. And lordy, but those V-shaped muscles at the top of his pants were the best kind of distraction.

Adam cleared his throat and my eyes shot to his. "You gonna stand there all night staring?" He smirked before he ordered, "You should get out of those wet clothes before you get sick."

I arched an eyebrow. "I bet you say that to all the girls." But he was right. My teeth were practically chattering, but I'd happily freeze to death if I got the chance to look him over all night.

His face was serious. "Never. I've never brought a girl to my home besides Raven."

"Seriously?" I was the only girl he'd ever brought here to meet his dad and see his room? Why? How?

"Yep, now get changed."

He turned around to give me some privacy and I slipped out of my wet clothes and slid his on. They smelled like him and all of a sudden, I had the urge to roll around in a pile of his clothes. God, he even smelled sexy. I was in so much trouble.

He picked my dress up off the floor and hung it over the back of a chair that sat at a small desk adjacent to his bed. "Will you get in trouble for not being home? It's getting late."

"I don't even think they know I'm gone." I'd long since given up caring if they cared.

His face said it all. That he thought that sucked, but instead of giving me any shit about it, he turned off the light and grabbed my hand and led me to the bed. He lay down and patted the spot next to him and I was so excited to be in his room and about to lie in his bed that I almost missed it. I almost didn't see all the glow in the dark stars and planets and constellations that covered his walls and ceiling.

"Ohh my goodness. It's beautiful." I spun around the room, arms out, feeling like I was floating in space. It was pitch-black and all I could see were the radiating stars and planets. It was one of the coolest things I'd ever seen.

"Come on. It's almost like the field," he said, patting the bed beside him, and I thought he was crazy because it was a hell of a lot better.

I crawled over to him, my wet hair hanging around my face. He was lying in the middle of the bed and I wondered where the heck he wanted me to lie if he was taking up the whole dang thing.

"Here," he said, patting his chest and I felt my face warm. I didn't let my shyness keep me from practically climbing his body like a tree and settling my head into the crook of his neck, my face into the solidness of his chest. He wrapped his arms around me and bent a leg until my leg fell between his and I was practically straddling his thigh.

"Mmm," I moaned because it felt good and not just in the arousing way. It had been a long time since someone had held me and it had never been someone who wasn't my immediate family.

I felt his chin at the top of my head. It made me happy and I sank further into him, my body going limp like a noodle. All the fight and gusto from earlier was gone and in its place was peace. "I love your room."

It was a little slice of beautiful heaven in that ugly building. On a scary side of town. It was totally Adam. His room was like a beacon of light in the dark. Just like him.

"Thanks. My mom helped me do it."

I wanted to ask how she'd died. What had happened, but instead I asked an easier question for him to answer. "What was she like?"

His answer was quick. "She was amazing. Her name was Jennifer, but my dad always called her Jenny. She had long, curly, blond hair and blue eyes."

That explained Adam's gorgeous blue eyes.

"She was a vegetarian and loved doing yoga and being outdoors. Pops used to call her a hippy jokingly, but she didn't care what anyone thought of her. She was quiet and awkward and prone to bouts of depressions, but she loved the stars and she loved to tell me about them."

I wrapped my arms around his torso. "She sounds wonderful."

"She was." It was just a whisper, but I still heard it long and clear. I felt like that whisper was a plea. A plea to talk about what happened. I felt like he was begging for someone to know and understand.

"What happened?" I murmured into his chest.

I felt his neck and chest work with grief under my head. "She killed herself. Pills. I found her one day when I got home."

My body locked tight at the news. No. I couldn't fathom that Adam had lost someone in that way and my heart completely broke for him. I couldn't imagine either of my parents leaving me willingly. I couldn't even fathom him finding her. Tears sprang to my eyes and I was so very sorry I'd even asked.

"How old were you?"

"Nine."

"Oh, God, Adam. I am so sorry," I choked out and I thought I felt a kiss pressed to the top of my head.

"It's okay. It's been a long time. She'd always struggled with depression. She used to work on the island, ya know? Cleaning houses."

"Really?"

"Yeah. She didn't have a degree or anything like that, but she liked taking care of others so it was a good gig for her. Until one of her employers assaulted her. That was the beginning of the end. She never got over it."

My head shot up off his chest and I stared down into intense azure eyes. "What? Like sexually?"

"Yeah."

"Jesus. That's awful."

"Yeah. She wasn't the same after that. She just never got over it. Never got any better. No matter how many therapist appointments she went to. No matter how many meds she took. No matter how my dad tried to protect her. She stopped leaving the house even to see the stars. She was just too soft, too tender-hearted. Too sensitive. It broke her."

God, my chest felt like it had been split wide-open. I was shattered for Adam and his sweet dad. And for his mother who'd experienced something so horrific.

"And the person who did it? What happened?"

Adam looked away from me and stared at the wall adjacent from us, his face speaking volumes. "What usually happens when someone from the island hurts one of us. Nothing."

"Nothing?" I sat up, feeling outrage, anger, hurt, too many damn feelings to count on this family's behalf. "Nothing?" My voice was getting louder.

Violence and injustice colored his features. "Don't you get it, Liv? Money gives people power. Control. We have no money over here, but over there you guys are swimming in it. You have all the power and meanwhile we suffer. We pay."

I didn't like how he lumped me in with them because I may have lived over there, but it wasn't a choice. I was still a kid. I wasn't one of them. I was just me. Livingston Rose Montgomery. Daniel Montgomery's only daughter. Lover of the stars. Obsessed with Adam Nova. I didn't care or know anything about the inner workings of that island and all of its money.

I pulled away, feeling guilty for some reason for something I had absolutely nothing to do with. But was I guilty by association? Would the bridge that separated Adam and me be the very thing that kept us apart?

"No. Don't do that."

"Do what?" I questioned, as I sat up, looking down at him.

"Pull away from me. I wasn't talking about you, Livvy. I was talking about them. *You* are not them."

I softened, letting out a long breath and lying back down. I was being irrational. It was a helpless feeling. I was just a kid. I couldn't change the world, much less that small island. I didn't want to talk about that anymore. It made me selfish, but it made me feel different than Adam. It made me feel like we were a million miles apart instead of lying in his bed together, so I changed the subject.

"Tell me how they met." I snuggled in. Pressing a kiss to the musky spot on his neck, I moaned a little.

"How who met?" he growled out like he was in pain, but I could tell by the flex of his stomach muscles under my hand that he was turned on by my kisses.

"Your mom and dad." I settled in and gave the poor guy a break. My guess was I wasn't his first anything and I wasn't quite sure if I was ready to take the next step with him.

I tilted my chin and looked up at him in the dark. I saw the small curve of his lips and thought I was really enjoying seeing him smile lately. It didn't seem like he'd done much of that before we met, but now he smiled a lot at me. It made me feel good.

"My dad loves to tell that story." Adam gave a small chuckle I felt through my entire body. "He's better at it, but I'll give it a go."

He got quiet, so I pinched his side. "Well, don't keep me in suspense, Nova."

"Okay!" he exclaimed, pulling my pinching hand

away and placing it palm down on his chest, right over his heart. "My dad used to work on cars before he got hurt. My mom was broke down on the side of the road, not far from here, so my dad stopped. He likes to say she was bent over the hood of the car and that he already knew he was going to marry her because she had the best ass in South Carolina."

He laughed and I giggled along. "He fixed her car and he asked for her number. She politely declined and so he wrote his name and number on a piece of paper and stuck it in the console of her car.

"Mom said she couldn't not call a gorgeous man who'd rescued her. Especially one with the last name Nova. A star. And with her love of astronomy she said it had to be fate."

I grinned like a fool into his chest. "That's so sweet."

"Mmmhmm. How did your parents meet?"

"It's definitely not as romantic as yours."

"So what? Tell me."

And so I did. We talked about my parents. About his friends. About his school and work. We spent the entire night wrapped in each other's arms until I fell asleep somewhere in the middle of a conversation about childhood animals.

It was one of the saddest and sweetest nights of my life. And definitely one I'd never forget.

CHAPTER 14

Adam

"Well, I'm just saying that if I were into girls, I'd totally date you," Liv said matter-of-factly, while smiling at Raven.

Raven was practically beaming, which made me grin at these two crazy girls. We were discussing Raven's non-existent dating life at the moment and her struggle to find a chick with substance.

"You would?" Raven said back. "Somehow I didn't think I was your type."

Liv looked taken aback before saying, "I have one type, Raven. Good. And I think you're plenty of that."

Raven gave me big eyes over her fries and ketchup. "Oh my God." She put her hand over her heart. "She's perfect." She looked up at the ceiling of the diner we were in. "Please God, if there is a perfect girl for him, there has to be one for me, right?"

I kicked her shin softly underneath the table and her eyes speared me with a playfully angry look. "What?

She's beautiful, funny, smart, and rich."

I grew sullen at the mention of Liv's money. I didn't like to talk about it. It was a point of contention between us, that island, her money. They seemed to be bigger than the bridge that separated the island from Madison. I didn't want to think about what her money meant for us or our future. What could I give her?

Liv didn't notice my turn of mood; she only laughed off Raven before saying, "Not yet. Remember, I don't get my money until I'm twenty-one. My stepmonster has all the control until then."

Raven was chewing on a piece of ice from her sweet tea when she answered, "That blows."

"Eh." Liv shrugged like it was no big deal. That was her general attitude about her family even though I knew they weren't the nicest to her. She had a dreamer's attitude. It baffled me. After all she lost. And with her circumstances now, she somehow still managed to dream. I'd given up on that long ago. My dreams had fallen by the wayside when my mom decided she didn't even have the will to live much less dream anymore.

"Well, we better get going." I loved hanging out with Raven and Liv together. Since the night at my house a few weeks ago we didn't just hang out at the field. Most of the time I went and got Liv from her house after everyone went to bed. She'd text me when she thought it was safe and I was happy to make sure she made it safely to the field and some nights, like tonight, we even managed to meet Raven for a late dinner while she worked at the diner across the street from the tattoo parlor.

"Yeah." Raven stood up and scooted out of the booth across from us. "It's time for me to get back to work anyway. I have a client." She moved her brows up and down.

"I take it she's hot?" Liv asked.

"Mmmhmm," Raven answered. "She has great tits."

"Jesus," I interjected, my face going hot.

Raven pursed her lips. "You didn't mind talking about tits with me before Liv started coming around."

Christ. Liv giggled and I rushed her out the door with my hand to the small of her back while Raven cackled behind me.

Everyone hugged, the girls twice, and Liv and I started our walk back to the field, her blue blanket tucked under my arm, her hand in mine. We were quiet as we made the walk. It was in that very second I realized what was happening, with her hand in mine, our silence was speaking volumes. I had a fucking girlfriend. I had gone from watching this girl like a crazy person to following her home and now look at us. We were walking hand in hand through my neighborhood. Liv was my girlfriend. I passed her the blanket that was under my arm and reached into my pocket for my smokes and lighter.

I needed a damn cigarette STAT. It wasn't that I was upset or mad about the prospect of Liv being mine. I loved that she was mine. It just scared the absolute shit out of me.

Liv gave me a disappointed look at the sight of the cigarette dangling from my mouth, but desperate times called for desperate measures. She didn't say anything, though. She just kept walking silently and I wondered if maybe that was because she knew. She knew how hard this was for me. To let her in. And that was just a whole other level of frightening because that meant she already knew me too well.

Fuck. I walked faster with her hand in mine, puffing away, hoping to ease the panic flaring throughout my body. We got to the field and she placed the blanket down gently until it was flat and ready for us to lie on.

She lay down and watched me pace a bit, still silent. And, jeez, I kind of wanted her to ask what was wrong, but it was pretty plain she already knew.

I put out my cigarette and stood right over her, staring. She was looking at the sky until she stopped and her eyes met mine. And instead of questioning what I was doing there, she held her hand out to me. Her small hand with pink nails. They were pretty and dainty and sweet. I couldn't resist. I sat down on the blanket and lay back. As soon as I was settled her hand made its way to mine. She wasn't slow and sweet with her hand-holding. She didn't question it. She snatched my hand up quickly and brought it to her chest before covering my hand with her other as well.

And just like that, my heart slowed. My panic receded and my skin buzzed with a warmth that made my head light. God, how did she know? How did this girl know what I needed even when I didn't?

I looked over at her, but her eyes were closed, so I took the opportunity to stare. Because how often in life did I get to just look at someone beyond beautiful without them knowing?

Her round cheeks were pink from the walk and her silky brown hair feathered around her head and brushed my cheek. It was the softest thing I'd ever felt in my life and it smelled so good. I wanted to kiss her small, button nose. To taste her wide pink lips.

She was stunning, breathtaking, and she was making me a romantic fool.

She had on a pink shirt that was really nothing more than a band of fabric around her torso. There were no sleeves to be seen and damn if she didn't have beautiful collarbones and shoulders. And her generous breasts, she seemed to be putting them on display as much as possible for me lately and if her cleavage was anything to go by, tonight was no exception. They rose and fell with every breath and it was so tempting. She was teasing a starving man and it wouldn't be long before I snapped and ate my fill.

"Close your eyes, Nova." Her words snapped me out of whatever lust-induced daze she'd put me in. Her eyes were still closed, but her lips were smiling.

"Why?" I wanted to watch her. She knew how I liked to watch.

Her grin widened at my question. "Because you can't dream with your eyes open."

I lifted up onto one elbow until my face was right above hers. I could practically taste her sweet breath. "I'm pretty sure I can," I whispered. Because my dreams had never compared to a moment I'd spent with her.

She was the dream. She was it for me.

Her eyes snapped open at my words and her smile was gone and in its place was a look of surprise. "What?"

I kissed her button nose like I'd been wanting to and smiled down at her. "Go out with me."

Her forehead scrunched in confusion. "I *am* out with…"

I shook my head. "No, Liv. Go out with me. Like I come pick you up and we go out. Somewhere special. Let me take you on a date."

"You wanna take me on a date?" Her words were a whisper and rang of disbelief. How could she not see it? How obsessed I was with her. How addicted I was to her lips. How my heart was only happy when it was with her.

"Yes."

She swallowed hard before answering. "Okay."

Okay. And I was good. Content. I lay back down next to her. She was staring at the stars and my eyes were glued to hers.

"What do you see when you look up there?"

She sucked her bottom lip into her mouth thoughtfully before answering, "A million possibilities. A world of aspirations, hopes, wishes." She turned her gaze to mine. "What do you see?"

I shrugged my shoulders. "Science." It was easy. So matter-of-fact, my answer.

Her face fell. "That's it?"

I looked at the sky again. "And darkness."

I could see her smiling at me from the corner of my

eye. She sat up and leaned forward until her face was close to mine. "Ah, but there can't be darkness without light, Adam."

Grabbing my hand, she lay back down. She made me feel lighter. Better. Bigger. Brighter. I smiled like a loon. She quietly watched the stars and I quietly watched her for a while.

Finally, she looked over at me and squeezed my hand, giving me a confounded look. "What are you doing over there?"

She knew what I was doing. She knew I was watching her. But I knew I was doing more than that.

And even though I felt hot and embarrassed at the truth, I stared into her eyes and gave it to her anyway because she deserved it. "Dreaming."

Her face was red and she was lit from within. "Oh, no. You can't do that."

"Do what?" I asked, sitting up again to stare down at her.

Biting her lips, she answered, "Don't you go getting better than you already are, Nova. I don't think my fragile sixteen-year-old heart can handle it."

I could see the reflection of a hundred tiny stars in her eyes. My heart felt like it might burst right open. "You ain't seen nothing yet, Montgomery." And I kissed her like my life depended on it.

CHAPTER 15

Liv

"Girl, what has been going on with you lately? You have missed two etiquette classes and have been late to school three times the last three weeks." Olivia Drake, robot girl, was following me down the hallway at school and grilling the hell out of me.

"I've been busy. It's not a big deal." I stopped at my locker and opened it.

Her lips pursed. "Ms. Donnelly didn't think it wasn't a big deal. You should have seen her face when you weren't at dance last night."

I almost smiled at how happy I was not to see her face last night. Instead, I'd snuck out to hang with Raven and Adam. It was a much better time than robot girl stepping on my toes.

"She was pissed and she is going to lose it if you don't show up today. Just wanted to give you a heads-up," she said, pushing off the locker next to mine and joining a group of girls walking down the hallway.

I let out a long breath, thankful she was gone.

"What did perfect princess want?"

I jumped at Mel's voice, surprised to see her behind my open locker door. I slammed it and turned to her. "Jesus, you scared the crap out of me."

I put my math book in my bookbag and slung it over my shoulder as we walked down the hall.

"So?"

"So what?"

"What did she want?"

"Oh, to warn me that Ms. Donnelly is pissed at me."

She laughed. "She totally is."

I smirked. "Oh, well." And I truly felt that way. I would be fine at the ball. I didn't need classes on how to be a Southern lady. I was already a Southern lady, damn it.

We walked out of the school and started the walk to etiquette. I wouldn't miss it today. I didn't need Ms. Donnelly tattling on me to crazy Georgina.

"So, spill it. Where the hell have you been lately? You never miss class and you've never been late for school."

I grinned. I couldn't help it. I was so excited about Adam. I wanted to tell someone. I wanted to shout it from the rooftops. And Mel was the closest thing I had to a best friend. I'd confided things to her in the past like Georgina's crazy and Sebastian being a creep. I couldn't help myself. I wanted to spill all the beans about Adam.

"Is it a boy?"

And I was done. I couldn't hold it in any longer.

"Yes," I squeaked out on a giggle like the schoolgirl I was.

"Oh my God!" she screeched and we took a moment to jump up and down in the road while holding hands.

When we finally calmed, she said, "Lordy, girl. Now you really do have to spill and you only have about fifteen minutes to do it before class starts, so tell me everything. I want all the deets!"

"Well, I have a date coming up. This weekend." I was totally bragging, but oh well. I was dying to spill my guts about anything and everything Adam Nova.

"Who is he? Where is he taking you?"

"I don't know! He says it's a surprise and you don't know him. I met him on the mainland."

Her smile fell. "What were you doing over there?"

"I don't know. Sometimes I go over there."

Her eyes narrowed on me. "How long have you been seeing him? How do you know he's safe?"

She didn't look happy for me. No, she didn't look pleased at all.

"We've been seeing each other for a few weeks." I was being purposefully vague. I didn't need her to lecture me or to feel disappointed that I hadn't told her the moment I met Adam.

We were almost to Ms. Donnelly's front door so when she paused on the steps, I stopped, too.

"You've only known this boy weeks and now you're going on a date with him? On the mainland? And it's a surprise?" She shook her head back and forth. "That doesn't sound safe to me, Liv."

Grabbing her hand, I pulled her the last distance to class, while saying, "It's fine, I trust Adam. He's a really nice, smart guy. You would like him, Mel."

Her lips pushed out and her eyebrows furrowed. "Adam? What's his last name in case you disappear and we have to look for you in the bottom of the ocean?"

I rolled my eyes. "Jesus, Mel. I didn't realize you could be this dramatic." To calm her the heck down I told her enough to get her off my back. "His name is Adam Nova and he goes to Madison Tech. He's a nerdy guy with a love for astronomy. I highly doubt he is going to throw me in the ocean."

I left out the smoking and tattoos and his general bad boy attitude. It was hard, too, because those tattoos were delicious and I wanted to shout from the rooftops how much I loved them.

"When is this surprise date?" She still looked skeptical as hell.

"Not until this weekend." And it was only Tuesday. It felt like forever.

"I don't know why you can't just date Braden. He's been mooning over you nonstop lately. And he's from the island and he's safe."

I didn't tell her that I felt safer with Raven and Adam than I did with the people here.

"Braden's not for me, Mel."

We walked up the steps to Ms. Donnelly's. Three other girls were standing on the porch, effectively cutting our conversation short. Which I was beyond relieved about. I was done discussing Adam. I wasn't going to stop seeing him. And I wasn't going to date Braden. The subject was closed.

"What are y'all doing out here?" Mel tried peering around them to Ms. Donnelly's front door.

"Guess class is canceled tonight. There's a sign on the door saying there was an emergency," Oliva robot child answered.

I pushed through the throng of girls. Sure enough there was a note on the door that said class would be tomorrow instead. Hell yes. My heart soared. I could go see Adam instead. He got out of class around five. I could head over that way and meet him at his place.

I pulled out my phone and shot off a text to him that I was on my way. Mel eyed me warily as I put my phone in my backpack.

"Off to see lover boy?"

"Yep." I popped the p on the word, effectively shutting her up.

I walked down the porch steps and headed for the bridge.

"Be safe, Liv." I heard called out from behind me.

I gave Mel the thumbs-up. I was surprised by her. She was always so spontaneous and definitely the bad girl of us two. I thought for sure she'd be supportive of me dating Adam. Her reaction was shocking and just didn't seem like her at all.

The sun was starting to set as I crossed the bridge. I sat in the middle of the bridge and watched the sunset a little before heading to the mainland. By the time I made it to Adam's, it was a little later than I thought it would be. I still hadn't heard back from him, so I tried opening the outside door, but it was a no go. It was locked from the inside. There was an old box on the outside of the building where you could dial up apartments. I hit the button for Adam's apartment but nothing happened. My guess was it was as busted as the rest of the building.

So, I sat on the front steps for over an hour, with no word from Adam. I kept myself entertained by doing my school work. I was deeply immersed in one of the classics for my literature class when someone sat down next to me, startling me to death.

"Well, look who it is." Boone's gray teeth smiled at me and I felt my breath catch. "I remember you. You're the girl from the field." His breath smelled like some kind of booze and I moved back out of his space and into the railing that ran up the side of the big porch. I'd already had one run-in with this awful man. Fear sliced through me that he had me alone this time.

He grinned wickedly. "What are you doing out here? Come looking for me?"

I stood up and tried to move down the steps, but he cornered me, pushing me back farther into the dark porch and under the small overhang.

My back was against the front door when I tried to answer with conviction. "I'm waiting on a friend." I was trying to sound like I wasn't terrified out of my mind, but I was pretty sure the waver in my voice gave me away because he gave me a sickeningly sweet grin that made my skin crawl.

"I bet you came over here to slum it with one of the mainland boys, huh? I bet those rich assholes from the island don't give you what you need." He pushed in until his face was an inch from mine and my body was plastered to the door behind me.

I pressed the side of my face against the door hard, but it didn't matter. He ran his nose up the side of mine. Adam had done the same the other night, but this was different. I was scared and weak and I had no control. I felt a single tear slip down my cheek.

"I bet you'd like me to fuck you right here against the door, wouldn't you, you dirty little slut? I know how you girls from the island like it."

My voice was frozen in my throat. I tried to scream out, to cry, but nothing would come out.

He tried to push his leg between mine, but I lifted my knee as hard as I could and nailed him in the balls. He grunted but still kept me pinned to the door and as hard as I pushed and scratched and hit, I was helpless. He was too big. Too strong, and I was too small, too weak.

"You're gonna pay for that, bitch."

Another tear slipped free as I remembered the night Adam had been so angry at me for going to Raven's late at night looking for him. It made sense now. It became all too clear in that moment. He was right. I was dumb.

Finally, my voice broke free and a wail filled the air as Boone's hand traveled up to my breasts, gripping one hard before savagely tearing the fabric at the top of my tank top. One side of my shirt hung open, revealing my bra beneath and I screamed out again. I pinched my eyes shut and with all my power I kicked out and yelled and punched and punched, tears pouring from my face, screams surging from my mouth.

All of a sudden, I was kicking and punching air. Confused, my eyes flew open and Boone was gone from the porch. All I could see was a blur of two bodies down on the sidewalk as I slid down the door onto my bottom. As the adrenaline left my body, my body shook. I'd never been so scared in my life.

The bodies on the sidewalk stopped and suddenly my brain registered what I was seeing. Adam was on top of Boone. His face was a red mask of rage. He had his forearm to Boone's throat. Boone's face was red and his eyes were bulging from his head, but he didn't seem to be fighting anymore.

"I will fucking kill you!" Adam screamed down at Boone, spittle flying from his lips.

I crawled to the edge of the steps, not trusting my wobbly legs. I had to help him. He was going to do something he would regret. And I couldn't let him do that. Not because of me.

Boone gurgled out sounds beneath Adam, but Adam was way past gone.

"I'm going to end you. You put your hands on her. You fucking put your hands on her!" he screamed into Boone's face.

"Please," I cried, trying to get his attention, but it came out a whisper, barely a breath. "Please," I tried again. I scooted down the steps as fast as I could and crawled over to Adam.

I placed a hand on his arm. "Please," I said again.

His head turned to me, but his forearm never let up against Boone's neck. His animalistic eyes landed on mine and at first I wasn't even sure he saw me. It was like he was in another place, another time.

I lifted my shaking hand to his cheek. "Hey, it's okay."

I watched as recognition slipped over his face, but it was quickly replaced with sadness. His face crumpled right before my eyes and even though I was in one of the most emotionally straining moments I'd ever experienced my heart went out to him.

His eyes filled with tears that would never spill over. His face was pure torture and devastation. "He touched you," he whispered and I rubbed my thumb along his high cheekbone.

Fresh tears spilled over and onto my cheeks.

"He put his hands on you," he growled. His eyes slipped over my shoulder and the ripped shirt there and his eyes went wild, his body locked tight with violence.

If possible, he pushed tighter to Boone's throat. "He hurt you!" he shouted.

"No," I cried. "I'm fine. I promise, I'm fine." I tried to soothe him.

But he turned his violent eyes to Boone and I had a feeling this was far from over. I stood up on shaky legs, prepared to do anything to stop Adam from what I knew was inevitably going to happen, but I didn't get a chance to do anything at all.

Sheriff Rothchild seemed to appear out of nowhere. "Go get in the car, Livingston," he ordered from beside me and then he was on Adam, pulling him from Boone, one arm around Adam's neck, the other around his waist.

I did not get in the car because fuck that. I stood there and made sure Adam was safe.

Boone scrambled back on the pavement, desperately trying to catch his breath. He coughed and wheezed and I might have felt terrible for him except that I knew in my heart of hearts he was evil and he had definitely planned to do more than just rip my shirt and scare me.

"Let me go!" Adam shouted at the sheriff, but Rothchild completely ignored him.

"Get in the goddamn car, Livingston!" he shouted at me instead of dealing with Adam.

I looked around for the sheriff's car and saw it about a block back, but I couldn't stand to leave Adam when he was in such a state.

"I can't," I whispered brokenly. "I need to make sure he's okay."

Meanwhile Adam was losing his damn mind. "Get the fuck off me!" he shouted at the sheriff. "Get your hands off me, you bastard!"

Boone got off the ground finally and made a run for it. The sheriff didn't seem to care too much about him getting away. He seemed more focused on Adam and my stomach turned at the thought of running into Boone again. Why didn't he go after Boone?

Sheriff Rothchild tossed Adam to the ground, holding him down. "Get in the car, Liv. I mean it. Right this minute. I'll take care of him."

I felt like I didn't have a choice, so I walked the block to the car, but not before I yelled back, "He wasn't hurting me! It was Boone! Boone was hurting me! He was protecting me!"

I watched Adam and the sheriff every step of the way. He didn't seem to be hurting Adam, but it didn't look like they were having a friendly conversation either. Adam was underneath him, and the sheriff was right in his face. Anger radiated from both of them as I got into the passenger side of the police cruiser.

I sat in the car for another two minutes, my hands shaking as I watched their interaction. I'd never forgive myself if Adam got into trouble for protecting me. It wasn't until the sheriff had pushed off Adam leaving him on the ground and walking back to the car that I wondered how Sheriff Rothchild had come upon us. As far as I knew, no one had called the cops or seen what had happened. And he hadn't arrived with sirens wailing. I was sure I would have seen and heard them. How had he found me?

Only one person knew I was seeing Adam. And I'd only told her mere hours ago. Anger ignited deep inside me. Was there no one I could trust? Was there no one on my side but my tattooed boy from the mainland? Was there no one who loved me left in the world? Betrayal blazed through me like the hottest fire. I vowed I wouldn't make such a crucial mistake again in being trustful and boastful.

Sheriff Rothchild opened the car door and slid into the driver's seat. He sat down with a heavy sigh and rubbed the heels of his hands into his eyes like he'd had a stressful night. *Yeah, me, too, man. Me, too.*

I pulled the top of my tank top up where it covered my bra and held it there while he cranked the car. He was quiet for about two minutes during the drive before he finally spoke. His words were careful, slow, almost calculated.

"I care about you, Livingston."

I didn't say anything because I didn't think he gave a shit about me, but I was Southern, so manners taught us if you didn't have anything nice to say, you didn't say anything at all. Besides, he'd kept Adam from killing Boone tonight, so I thought I owed him some grace.

"Georgina cares about you, too."

I huffed at that and he gave me a reprimanding look before turning back to look at the road.

"You don't belong on the mainland. It's not safe in North Madison. You got no business over there."

My back shot straight as I rolled my eyes. He was right in a lot of ways. It wasn't safe over there but nothing would keep me from Adam.

"I don't want you over there again. Your daddy wouldn't like it either. Do you hear me?"

Now that got my hackles up. How dare he use my daddy as a ploy to keep me from Adam? I wanted to tell him he didn't know shit about my daddy, but I just looked out the front window and pretended I didn't hear his question. I was seething.

And Mel. I'd only told her today, but it sure didn't take long for Mel to sell me out. I felt sick and devastated and so fucking sad in that moment. I had no one and now they were going to take Adam from me, too. I would be alone again. I couldn't bear it. More tears spilled over and onto my face. He was going to tell Georgina. She'd never let me out of the house again. I was a minor. I had no control.

"Do you understand me, Livingston?" It wasn't a question this time. It was an order. I felt like falling to a million pieces. The sweetness of the last several weeks shattered around me and I hiccupped back a sob.

As we crossed the bridge and entered the island, I felt like my heart was back on the mainland with Adam. I wondered if he was okay. I wanted to hug him. I wanted to hold him. I just wanted *him*.

When we got home that night I'd expected the sheriff to come inside and tell Georgina about the whole ordeal. But he didn't. He just dropped me at the front door, ripped tank top and all. I crumpled on the front porch right against the door and had a good cry. Not for me. Not for my ripped shirt. Not for my waning innocence. No, I cried for Adam Nova.

CHAPTER 16

Adam

How much could one hate their self? That's the question I asked myself every time I looked in the mirror. Was it not enough that I had to find my mother dead after suffering a sexual assault? Was it not enough that I couldn't help her and protect her? Was I also now supposed to endure the torture of knowing I couldn't protect the girl I loved, too? That's right. I fucking loved her. And I couldn't do anything to keep her safe.

I stared at myself in the bathroom mirror. I wasn't good enough for her. She didn't belong over here. And Sheriff Rothchild, as much as I hated his guts, he was right, I needed to stay the hell away from Liv. It was best for her. It was hell for me.

I touched the small cut on my lip. It stung, but I bet it didn't compare at all to the bruises Liv suffered on the inside. Every time I thought of the night before I felt sick, crazy—fucking violent.

I'd finished up my day at school and stayed at the

lab until dark to get some work done on a paper. My phone had been dead. I got angry every time I thought about that dead phone. It was my fault. Seeing her messages this morning when I'd finally charged it up and powered it on nearly killed me. She'd been there waiting for me. She'd gotten done early with classes and wanted to be with me.

And Boone. That fucker. I still wanted to kill him every time I thought of walking up the stoop of the apartment building and hearing Liv's scream. Something had come over me. Something I'd never be able to explain. Savage. That was the only word to describe me.

I'd ripped him off her, blind rage burning inside of me. I didn't even remember putting him to the ground or using my arm to choke him. It all seemed like a nightmare now. Seeing Liv's tear-stained face. Her begging me to stop. Her ripped shirt shredded my soul.

I hadn't protected my mother. And I hadn't protected her either. If she kept coming around here, it wouldn't be too long before her spirits were crushed, too. Before this place ate up every bit of her goodness and spat her soulless body out with nothing left. I couldn't let that happen. I had to protect her. From Boone. From Madison. From me.

My phone buzzed from the counter for what felt like the hundredth time today and I picked it up. It was no surprise to see Liv's name flashing across the screen. I was an asshole. A complete douche because she'd been messaging me since this morning and I hadn't answered. I didn't know how to tell her this couldn't go on anymore. That we had to end whatever this was.

Whatever this was. Like I didn't fucking know. But hell, I could pretend. I was good at that.

I looked at the phone again and pulled up the slew of Liv's texts I'd been avoiding all day.

Liv: Call me
Liv: Are you okay?
Liv: Can we talk?
Liv: Please talk to me

The last message made me want to tear my heart out and throw it off the bridge that would forever separate us and not just by distance. I debated what to do as I walked down the stairs and smoked a cigarette in front of the building. Just the sight of the porch made my stomach roll. No, no matter how I felt about her, I couldn't let her come back here. I couldn't risk her.

Pulling out my phone, I texted Liv back that I'd meet her at the beach across the street from her house in thirty minutes. Even at nineteen, I wasn't immature or dick enough to break things off with her over the phone. Besides, I had to see her. Just one more time.

I ran upstairs, praying I didn't see Boone's ass walking around. I didn't want to go to jail today.

I opened the door to the apartment, ready to shout to my dad I was heading out when I saw him sitting in a chair in the front room. "I'm heading out for a bit, Pops."

The gauze was gone from his forehead and he was

looking better. I felt relieved. He was all I had left. I had to take good care of him.

"You headed to see Liv?"

I nodded and searched for my house keys on the table by the front door.

"What are you love birds getting up to tonight?"

I tried to smile. I really did. I didn't want to burden him with this. "Just the beach."

He nodded and then I saw his eyes zero in on my lip. "What happened to your lip, *hijo*?"

"Nothing, Pops. It's fine. Just some bullshit between Boone and me."

My dad didn't miss a damn thing. He was a good father despite our shitty circumstances. "Did this thing with you and Boone have anything to do with Livingston?" His eyes were like an X-ray machine. Sometimes I thought he could see right through me.

I looked around the room. Anywhere but at him. Because if he asked me about what happened between me and Boone and I had to tell him about Liv, I knew I would lose it. I'd cry like a fucking baby. And I didn't have time to cry. To fucking care. I needed to make a clean break and move on with my life. It was best for everyone.

"I see you're not ready to talk about it. But when you are, I'm here. Okay?"

I still didn't look at him. I only nodded and grabbed my keys and flew through the door like a bat out of hell. I was careful to watch out for Sheriff Rothchild. I didn't need him breathing down my neck any more than usual.

I made it to the beach in record time. I was five minutes early, but it didn't matter because she was already there. She was sitting on the dunes, looking out at the ocean. I stood there and watched for a few moments, knowing this could be the last time I saw her. The last time I could watch her.

The sun was setting over the ocean, but I hardly noticed it. Her long beautiful brown hair whipped around her face. She was wearing a baggy white T-shirt and black leggings. Her bare feet were pressed into the sand and she looked so sad staring out at the ocean.

Fuck. Here goes nothing.

My Converse kicked up sand as I walked toward her. I could tell the moment she knew I was there. Her body locked tight as she turned her head to the side to watch me walk toward her. She got to her feet and ran at a dead sprint right for me.

Before I knew what I was doing she was in my arms and I was holding her to me, my hands around her waist. Her legs around mine. She pulled me close and buried her face in my neck. Her body shook against mine. She cried into my neck and I couldn't stand it. I came here to break up with her. To say goodbye to my very first girlfriend. The girl I thought I might love. And instead I ran my hands down her back and rocked her from side to side.

I sat in the dunes, her still wrapped around me like a warm blanket. "Shhh." I pushed her hair out of her face and whispered into her ear. I couldn't stand it. Her pain killed me.

When she finally calmed down, she leaned back on my knees and kissed my lips softly. Her hands framed my face and she rubbed the scruff along my jaw.

"You're hurt," she whispered, pressing a kiss to the tiny cut on my lip.

Grabbing her hands, I shook my head. "No, I'm fine."

"I'm sorry," she muttered.

I pulled her close again, hugging her tight, cradling her in my arms. "It's not your fault."

"It is," she said into my chest.

I pulled her back until she could see my face. The seriousness. So she could understand what I was saying was the damn truth. "It was Boone's fault. And mine. I didn't protect you." I felt my jaw tick as I faced the inevitable. What I'd known was always coming since the very beginning.

It was dark now, the stars coming out to play.

I stared at them as she spoke. "It's not your fault. You warned me to be safe."

"It doesn't matter," I said to the sky. "We can't do this anymore." I blinked back all the emotion about to spill over.

She backed out of my embrace until she was perched on my knees, straddling my legs. "This? We can't do this anymore?"

I couldn't look at her. I wouldn't. It would obliterate my already broken heart.

But she wouldn't let me be. Grabbing the sides of

my face hard in her hands, she made me look into her eyes. "This? You mean us? Do you mean us? Is that what you mean by *this*?"

I squeezed my eyes closed. I couldn't look at the hurt in hers for one more second.

"No, open your eyes while you break my heart, Adam. It's only fair."

I lifted my eyelids slowly. Her face ravaged my soul.

I didn't know what to say. I knew nothing would make her understand. Hell, I knew what had to happen, but even I had a hard time understanding life was so fucking unfair. So, I gave her all I had, which was my truth.

"I can't protect you." The words were like saw dust in my mouth, thick and dry.

She shoved my chest. "You don't have to."

"We're from two different worlds. It's never going to work out. Hell, it's only been two months and it's already not working out." God, I was lying. The last two months had been amazing. It was going to kill me to give her up.

Now she just looked angry. "What? Because of Boone? You're going to give me away because of one night with one bad guy?"

I had to make her see. My world was full of bad guys. I grabbed the tops of her arms, giving her a shake. "Don't you get it?" I shouted, my voice cracking with emotion. "The world is full of bad people, Liv. Those people will never let us be."

And she didn't even know the half of it. It wasn't

just the people on the mainland who would keep us apart.

She shoved off me and stood, staring down at me like she didn't even know who I was. It was like a hot iron to my soul. *I'm the first man who has kissed you. The first man to touch you. I'm yours and you're mine*, I wanted to scream, but I couldn't. Because we were over.

"See, that's where we're different, Adam. I'd never let anyone keep you from me."

I pushed off the ground, pissed off, too, now. "That's not fair."

She walked up to me and stood toe to toe. Head to head. Heart to heart. "You know what's not fair? You giving up on me. On us. That's not fair."

She wounded me through and through. I wanted to hug her. I wanted to shake her. She wanted me to fight for us, but I couldn't because I was too busy fighting for her. I'd be miserable the rest of my days if it meant she was safe and happy.

I swallowed what felt like sand in my throat and looked at the stars. They looked different tonight. Not quite as bright. Not quite as beautiful. "You and I, Liv? We're just not written in the stars," I choked out the lie. It left a horrible taste in my mouth.

But she had an answer for everything. "Then we'll rewrite them."

Everything was so easy for her. My Luna, the dreamer. "I can't," I whispered.

"You can't what?" Her beautiful brown eyes shimmered with tears as they stared up at me.

"I can't risk you. I'm scared. I can't lose you." I felt like I was drowning in the ocean in front of me even though I was safe on the sand.

Her head shook back and forth slowly before her hand came up and cradled my jaw so delicately it was like she was afraid I might break.

"So, you'll throw me away instead? I'm not her, Adam. I'm not her. I don't need saving. I just need you."

My forehead fell to hers as I let out a long breath I felt like I'd been holding for years. How did she know? How did this woman-girl somehow put a voice to all my fears? But she was right, she wasn't my mother.

"I know," I whispered across her lips.

Her doe eyes gazed at me from behind her eyelashes. Those eyes were a killer and almost impossible to say no to. They'd be the demise of us both.

"We're gonna be fine as long as we stick together." She ran her hands through my hair and I closed my eyes. I fucking melted.

"It's you and me, Nova. You and me against the world."

She didn't know how right she was. I ran my nose along the length of hers, breathing in her fresh scent. I was pretty sure that was what innocence smelled like, but I couldn't be sure. I'd never been this close to it.

I wanted her. I couldn't give her up, no matter how I knew it was the right thing to do.

"Kiss me," she whispered and that was it. That request was all it took.

My hand went to the back of her neck and up and

into her loose hair. I clenched it in my hands and turned her head the way I wanted it. How I needed it.

Pressing my mouth to hers, I groaned. Tasting her, kissing her like I'd been waiting to do for what felt like forever. I held nothing back. I bit and sucked at her lips. I devoured her mouth right to the edge of something that felt like insanity. I pushed her down onto her back and crawled over her, settling into the sweet spot between her thighs. She was deliciously warm there and her heat cradled my length too perfectly.

"Can I?" I whispered across her lips, my eyes eating her up. I couldn't stop myself. I was a wild man. I didn't even know what I was asking her. Could I what? Kiss her? Taste her? Love her? Keep her?

My eyes darted from her bare midriff where her shirt had ridden up to the tops of her supple thighs and back up to pass over her breasts, and on to the soft curve of the spot where her neck met her throat. That soft, fragrant spot where I wanted to bury my face and breathe her in. My mouth watered. My body craved hers. I was starving and only Liv could fill me up.

Her torso made a beautiful arch, her breasts pushing into my chest, her body needing me like mine needed hers. "Please," she begged.

That one word and I was gone. I may as well have been a thirteen-year-old boy again. I wanted to be brash, immature. I wanted to rush. I wanted to take and pillage and steal every bit of her she wouldn't willingly give me. God, I wanted to be selfish and kiss her and taste her like the crazy man I was being. I sucked in a shaky breath, trying to gain a little sanity, a little fucking composure. Slowly, carefully I pushed up her shirt over her breast, baring the sweetness of a lacy white bra, a small bow in the middle that made me ravenous. I was bad for her. That bow was proof. She was sweet. She was covered in lace and small bows and me, I was covered in dark ink and despair. It was wrong, but it felt right and so fucking good.

My finger traced that bow and above it, right between the milky, white globes that begged for my mouth. But I took my time. There'd only be one time that I'd get to see her beautiful body for the first time. Only once ever that I'd get to experience all of our first times. I didn't want to forget a single one. I wanted them all tucked away for the time she finally realized I wasn't worthy of her. That we'd never work. Me from the wrong side of the bridge, her from the right. Everyone against us.

Looking into her deep brown eyes and sweet face, I couldn't help but wonder what if. What if I didn't live on this side of the bridge? What if she didn't live on the island? What if I was good enough for her? What if our pasts and presents hadn't collided like a head-on collision? Just what fucking if.

At that moment looking down at her with her eyes shimmering with want, her body flushed and hot, her lips pink from mine, it seemed like so much more than a mere bridge separated us. It seemed like we were worlds apart. Universes even. She was so beautiful. And I was just me. Adam Nova. Poor introverted kid, scared of people, terrified of success, frightened of failure, angry at my circumstances. What did I possibly have to offer this angel? Not a goddamn thing, but that didn't stop me. Nothing would.

I still took. It was all I knew how to do. So, I leaned down, capturing her mouth in a blistering kiss that made the cheeks of my face hurt she was so sweet. The kiss was just that good. I was so fucked.

"Jesus, you're so beautiful," I groaned, taking her lips again, tasting every corner and crevice of her mouth with my tongue and God, she was good. Better than anything I'd ever tasted before. She moaned and I swallowed it down, desperate for her sounds. I wanted it all. I wanted her. Fuck, but life wasn't fair.

I felt her warm hands in my hair and then the sides of my face, her skin hot against mine before they slid down to cover the tattoos at my neck. I paused and stared down, our eyes meeting like they'd done it a thousand times before, our souls impossibly twisted together.

"You're beautiful, too."

Heat enveloped my face even as my heart tripled its beat. Nobody had ever called me beautiful. The world couldn't love you if you hid from it. But Liv, she saw me. Through my tattoos. Through my quirks. Through my shadows. She didn't mind my introversions. She saw me when no one else did. And she thought I was beautiful, even with all my flaws.

I buried my face in her sweet spot at the base of her neck, careful to hide the emotion I knew was shining in my eyes. And she let me hide, because she knew I needed it. She just knew. Always.

I wouldn't take. I'd give. It was what she deserved. If I took, then I'd want to keep her forever and Livingston Montgomery was not anything I could keep. She was on loan from the universe like my own walking, talking miracle.

I blinked back the wetness in my eyes and dipped my tongue into the indentation above her collarbone, making her shiver. I smiled against her shoulder before moving lower, right above that bow. I licked her slow and long from the top of it to the divot in her neck.

I was in heaven, having her. I was in hell knowing I couldn't keep her.

Settling myself between her legs, I slid my hand in the waistband of her stretchy pants that hugged her ass too well. "Yeah?" I asked, looking down at her, unsure, still shocked she wanted me like I wanted her.

Her eyes dropped closed as a "Please," fell from her lips. And me? I nosedived into oblivion. I was lost. Her scent in my nose, her skin on my skin, her heart pressed to my own. She was too good to be true.

I pulled the strap of her bra down as my other hand slid into the dampness hidden beneath her panties. And Jesus, it was wet. So wet. So ready for me. I groaned, pulling the rest of the strap down and exposing the dusky pink of her nipple, hard and ready for my mouth. I took it, sucking deep as my finger slid further into her wetness. Her hands tight in my hair, she arched her body, begging me without words. I found her hot core and swirled my finger there, testing, making sure I wouldn't hurt her, my cock the hardest it had ever been against the zipper of my jeans. I wanted to rip them off and press the head of it there, right at her center.

"God, please." She pulled my hair harder and tried to ride my hand. "Please, put it in. Touch me. Do something. Anything," she breathed.

Fuck anything. I wanted to do everything.

"Shhh," I quieted her, crooning against her breast, afraid someone would hear her even though I was sure this stretch of the beach was empty save us. But those sounds, those words, they were for me alone. They were mine. She was mine, if only for this moment, if only in this place.

I slid my finger in and it was so tight and hot, I almost came right there. Right there beneath our stars, with my pants still on. Fuck, but she felt good.

Moving up her body, I dropped kisses to the tops of her breast, the slope of her jaw, the tip of her nose, my hand stroking her—my heart on my sleeve.

I pressed my forehead to hers and slid my finger to the hilt, filling up her tight space. And when I pressed my thumb to her clit, her eyes flew open, meeting mine on a gasp.

"How does it feel?" I whispered against her lips, circling her while I moved my finger in and out slowly, determined to feel as much of her as I could. I won't lie, knowing I was the only man who'd ever touched her, to know I would be the first man to ever make her come, it made me crazy.

She gasped and clutched at me and held my wrist against her, riding my fingers.

"How does it feel, Liv?" I ran my tongue along the Cupid's bow of her lip. "Tell me," I demanded. Gone was my fear, my reservations, and in their place was need and want.

Her lusty eyes met mine head-on. "It feels like flying," she gasped and bowed her back. "Oh God," she groaned, pushing my hand harder into her. "It feels like falling."

And then I watched her fall. She shook in my arms and her core clamped tight around my hand. I made sure to rub my thumb to her, bringing her down slowly, but sure to draw out every bit of goodness I could.

The skin of her chest glistened with sweat and I leaned down, tasting it.

"Mmmm," she moaned, sounding satisfied and even though I'd just made her come all I could think about was putting my mouth between her legs and my cock in my hand and making her come again. This girl. She was going to be the damn death of me. She was a game changer. I didn't know it then. But I sure as hell knew it now.

CHAPTER 17

Liv

My hands shook a little as I put lip gloss on my lips. I was thirty minutes early. I sat on my bed and slipped on a pair of brown booties. I had no idea where Adam was taking me tonight. I only knew he was taking me on a date and I was beyond excited. It was my first real date and I was nervous as hell, but if it was anything like our evening on the beach a few nights ago, I was all in.

That night things had changed. Our relationship had grown, despite Adam trying to break things off with me. He'd opened up. He'd confessed his greatest fears and I'd known since that night in his apartment when he'd told me about his mom why Adam hid. He didn't want to be hurt. He didn't want to lose anyone again. You couldn't lose people you loved if you didn't open your heart enough to love them in the first place.

I stood in front of the mirror in my room and pulled down on the bottom of my denim dress. It was short but that was the point, wasn't it? I wanted to look sexy for Adam, especially after our night on the dunes. Harry stood in the mirror next to me.

"How do I look, bud?" I raised my eyebrows at him in the mirror.

One of his ears popped up and he whined a bit.

"I'll take that as I look amazing," I mumbled more to myself than to the dog.

Since our night in the dunes I found myself worried Adam was going to break things off with me. That day, I'd been so happy to see him unharmed. I'd launched myself into his arms, my relief palpable. And he'd crushed it, crushed me with his words. I knew he was scared. I was scared, too, but I was willing to risk it all. I could only hope Adam was, too.

The dunes. God, I'd never felt like that. Sure, I'd touched myself, but having someone you loved touch you, that was a completely different thing.

I paced around the room nervously. Stopping in my tracks, I realized my thoughts. Oh my God, did I love Adam? Oh my God, I did. I loved him and now all I could think about was him touching me again.

Or me touching him. Yes, that sounded good, too. And I had to admit I looked good tonight. A vast improvement from the hoodies and leggings I'd been sporting when I wasn't in my school uniform.

I'd spent the last couple of days skipping out on etiquette classes and totally hiding from Mel. I wasn't ready for the inevitable confrontation I knew I had to have with her. She'd done me dirty. I would've never ratted her out like that. Part of me didn't even understand why she'd done it. All I knew was that I was beyond thankful that Georgina and Sebastian weren't home now. There would most likely be a throw down if they were, because I was going on a date with Adam Nova come hell or high water.

I wore my hair in a thick braid to the side, fussed with it and checked to make sure my mascara hadn't run. I wasn't big on makeup or dressing up usually, but I really wanted to look good for my first date and for Adam.

He was supposed to pick me up any minute and I wondered where we were going and what we would be doing since he'd said he'd wanted to surprise me. I knew nothing except that he would come here to get me. He'd insisted since it was a date.

The doorbell rang and I checked my teeth in the mirror to make sure there wasn't any pink gloss on them. I grabbed my purse and headed down the stairs on shaky legs, Harry at my heels. I was nervous as heck.

I didn't know why. I'd been out with Adam lots of times, but this felt different. It felt big.

I teetered on my booties as I answered the door. The humid air hit me as I swung the door wide, but it wasn't the heat that took my breath away. There he stood. The boy who starred in all my fantasies. Only he looked better than he did in my dreams.

He'd clearly brushed his dark hair off his head and gelled it back off his face so I could really see his stunning blue eyes. They took me in from head to toe while my eyes ate up the length of him, all the way from his black leather jacket to the white T-shirt underneath and down to his dark denim jeans he wore like a second skin. I wondered how he got in them, all the while wondering how I would get in them. My cheeks were pink at the thought as I stared at the same black knock-off Docs he always wore.

"Jesus. You're trying to kill me."

It was like he could read my mind.

I looked up and his warm eyes were on my legs. It was like they were touching me. Goose bumps broke out on my thighs. I grinned. "No, I like you too much to kill you."

"Thank God," he said, stepping forward and wrapping his arms around my waist. "Because then I couldn't do this." He kissed my forehead and then my nose before finally getting to my lips.

I opened for him eager to taste him. It had felt like days when in reality I'd just kissed his face off last night in our spot under the stars.

He backed out of our kiss, smiling, and I felt like it was heaven on earth, seeing Adam smile like that. He hardly smiled at all when we first met. And, man, he smelled delicious.

"You smell good," I mumbled into the front of his jacket. I breathed in the scent of leather and smoke and some of the most amazing cologne I wanted to bathe in. I pulled at the collar of his jacket. "You dressed up for me."

He bit his lip and his eyes flirted with me. Grabbing my hand, he pulled me through the door and down the steps to where an old Honda Accord sat parked in the driveway.

"Where did you get a car?"

Adam didn't drive and neither did his dad. They took the public transportation everywhere or walked.

"It's on loan from Raven." He tapped the top of the car and opened the door for me. I slid in, feeling on top of the world. I had a sexy tattooed boy who opened car doors for me and put on cologne. He'd borrowed a car. He'd brushed his hair and gelled it. He liked me. A lot.

My stomach somersaulted as he closed the door to the car and walked around. I fidgeted with the bottom of my dress while he got in the car and cranked it up.

He glanced over at me before he very slowly leaned over until we were face-to-face. I thought he was going to kiss me senseless. Instead he backed away as he pulled the seat belt across my body and snapped it into place.

"Precious cargo," he muttered.

My heart melted into a big old fat puddle right in that seat.

"Where are we going?" I asked as we pulled out of the drive. I was giddy. So excited.

"I've already told you. It's a surprise."

I looked around the small car and noticed it was very well taken care of and ridiculously clean.

"Raven must love you to let you borrow her car."

He shrugged. "We've been friends most of my life."

"And Boone?"

His body locked tight at the mention of him and I

felt like a fool for mentioning him tonight. But it had just slipped out. After all, he'd been hanging with him that night in the field. In fact, that was the very first night we'd officially met.

"Boone isn't a friend. He was more of an acquaintance. And now he's dead when I finally see him again."

I turned in my seat and grabbed his hand from his knee and held it in mine. "I don't want you doing anything to him. You'll get into trouble. Let the police handle him. I'm sure Sheriff Rothchild is on top of it."

He scoffed and shot me an angry look before watching the road again. "Is that what you think, Liv? Really?"

I didn't understand. It was the police's job to protect us. Why would I think anything other than that? "I don't understand."

We pulled into a dark parking lot and Adam removed his seat belt and turned to me. My chin was nestled in the warmth of his palm. He ran his thumb over my lip. "You're sweet, baby. And innocent. Too innocent."

I pulled my chin out of his hand. He made it sound like a bad thing. My sweetness. "What does that even mean, Adam?"

"Nothing," he said gruffly, exiting the car.

He came around my side and opened the door and helped me out.

I leaned against the closed door, wanting answers even at the expense of my first date. "What does it mean? That I'm too innocent."

He leaned into me, kissing the tip of my nose like he so often did. "Nothing. I'm sorry. You're perfect just the way you are. I wouldn't change a hair on your head."

His eyes were sad, so I didn't question him further.

"Let's just have fun tonight, okay?" His words whispered over my lips.

I shivered as I nodded my answer.

He stepped back with a smile, but his eyes held a weariness that worried me. Opening the back door of the car, he waggled his brows and reached in, producing a cute white wicker picnic basket from the back seat.

"We having a picnic?" I asked as he held my hand and walked me toward a brick building with a round dome.

"Mmmhmm. A picnic under the stars."

He let go of my hand and reached in his pocket for a set of keys and started to open the door to the building.

"How can we have a picnic under the stars if we're going inside?"

His eyes were lighter now, sweeter. "You'll see."

And that's when I saw it, the sign for The Madison Planetarium.

"Oh my God!" I grabbed Adam's hand to stop him from opening the door. "We can't go in here. It's not open, Adam!"

He finished unlocking the door and held up the key ring, swinging it back and forth. "But I have a key," he said, grinning playfully.

I was terrified we were going to get in trouble. "How did you get a key?"

He opened the door and ushered me through with a hand to the middle of my back and his other hand carrying the white basket.

"You know, it's this crazy thing. Sometimes when you work somewhere, they give you a key. Ya know, so you can get in and out."

I stopped in what looked to be a huge reception area complete with shining marble floors, a customer service desk, and a huge planet that looked to be Saturn on the wall.

I was stunned. "You work here?"

I looked around the room, trying to picture him here, in this cool but totally fancy place, working. I felt like all of a sudden I didn't know him at all.

"Yeah. Since I was fifteen. Started sweeping the floors and shit. Now I run the school kids show in the mornings before I go to school."

He ran the school shows? I didn't even think Adam had a job. I thought he went to school and helped take care of his dad.

"School shows?" I looked at him, standing there all easy breezy, the basket dangling from his hand.

"Yeah, I do the live shows for the field trips in the mornings. I'm what they call a Sky Show Actor."

He rocked back on his heels and looked around the place like what he was telling me wasn't rocking my world. Like it wasn't the craziest, most unexpected, most amazing thing he'd ever told me about himself.

"You work here? And teach little kids about the stars?" I asked, dumbfounded.

He gave me a look that said he thought I was crazy. "Yeah?"

I honestly couldn't believe it. My tattooed, smoking, ill-tempered, one-word answering boyfriend working at a planetarium. Teaching children about the stars he loved so much.

You could have knocked me over with a feather. And if for one second I thought that I couldn't adore this boy any more than I already did I was dead wrong. Dead. Wrong.

But still, I wondered if we should be in here at night when the place was closed. I'd never dare jeopardize Adam's job, even for a really cool date.

I looked around the big room again and walked over to the mural of Saturn on the wall. "Are we even supposed to be in here?"

Adam grabbed my hand. "It's fine, Liv. I promise."

He walked me down a hallway that seemed to go on forever before we entered a domed room. I looked around, amazed at how big and dark it was.

He placed our picnic basket on the floor in the middle of the room. It seemed like a million chairs circled us in amphitheater seating. Reaching into the basket, he smiled at me before pulling out a blanket and laying it on the floor.

"Have a seat." He gestured to the blanket.

"I've never been to a planetarium," I rushed out excitedly.

"Really?" He seemed surprised.

I nodded as I sat on the blanket, making sure my

dress covered my behind.

He held up a finger. "I'll be right back."

He left me in the dark of the room for a few minutes. I wanted to peek through the basket, but I didn't.

The dome over my head lit up with a sky full of stars and it nearly took my breath away. I had no idea how real it would look. How up close it would appear. It was almost better than my field beneath the stars.

Adam returned and the show began. The stars moved sometimes seeming to come at us. Other times seeming to move away. One thing remained the same, I was enchanted. Adam pointed to the sky, his deep voice washing over me as he told me stories, legends, and myths about the stars.

I sometimes watched him in a daze. His passion, his love for astronomy was deeper than I had even realized. He was brilliant and astonishing and I didn't think I'd ever meet another man in my life who came close to Adam Nova. He was amazing and to think he'd been hiding all this time.

Sometime in the middle of his show, he pulled a fast food burger from the wicker basket and handed it to me. He uncapped an old school glass bottle of soda and passed it my way. It reminded me of his notes in the bottle and I smiled like a fool.

I ate my dinner and drank my soda while a million stars danced over my head to the sound of Adam's voice. It was the most perfect date ever.

And it only got better when Adam ended the show with, "Until the next time I see you beneath the stars."

I laughed in the middle of a sip of Coke and the bubbles burned my nose. "Oh my God. Do you say that every time?"

He grinned at me. "Every time."

I pretended a serious look. "And see, I thought that was just for me."

He closed the gap between us and brought his lips to mine. "It seems like everything I do lately is just for you."

"Yeah?" I whispered back, beyond flattered.

"Mmm," he moaned against mouth, tasting me. He pushed the wrappers and empty bottles away as he crawled over me. He never stopped kissing me through it all. They weren't the same as our kiss in the rain. They were methodical kisses peppered with a sweetness that seemed to be the general antithesis of Adam. But still, they didn't surprise me. I'd come to learn to never expect anything of Adam because most likely he'd prove you wrong. And sometimes in the best possible ways.

But I wanted the passionate kisses. The wild ones. Like our night in the rain. So I pressed my chest into his and ran my fingers through the back of his hair. That did the trick. He growled and kissed me hard, like I wanted.

And all of a sudden, we were two stars colliding. Electric. On fire. But like everything Adam did, he was slow. His licked the roof of my mouth. Bit my bottom lip. Sucked the sting. All the while his hands traveled the expanse of my thighs and up, until his fingers ghosted around the sides of my panties at my hip. He brushed the hair off my forehead and leaned back so he could look me in the eye.

"Okay?" he asked.

There wasn't a second that I questioned what he was asking.

I nodded and pulled his lips back to mine, the fever back and blazing through me like a wild fire in my veins. His knuckles brushed over my panties right at the apex of my thighs and I groaned.

"I like that," he muttered against my mouth. "I love you when you make those sounds." His words sounded slurred like he'd had too much to drink. But no, he was drunk on me.

My skin prickled, my hands shook. The place between my legs ached. If he was drunk on me, then I was high on him. I wanted. His hands swept my dress up and up some more until I felt cold air around my thighs. While he pushed my panties down, I lifted my hips, feeling the most powerful I'd ever felt in my life.

I felt like I was going to float right off the floor and into the starry sky above us, but the intensity of his stare kept me pinned firmly to the floor. I wanted. I craved.

I needed him to touch me. I wanted to feel him. Sliding my palm down the front of his chest, I kept my eyes glued to his. I'd never done this; touched a boy. But it didn't matter with Adam. I knew there wasn't a wrong way to do it. I kept going, past the bumps of his abs, the smoothness below. Slowly, so slow because I just innately knew that's how this boy would like it. I palmed him there. Right over his hardness. Soft at first. He blew out a hard breath that made me squeeze my thighs together. And then harder, until I was gripping the full length of him. Until he was moaning and I was moving my hand up and down and gripping over the denim of his pants and he was sweating and cussing.

"Fuck," he growled, his damp forehead to mine. "Jesus, I want you." The words tore from his throat.

"Well, then take me," I said, feeling strong, compelling, potent. I wasn't just high, I was flying. Some girls lost their virginity in the back of a truck out on a dirt road. Some on their small twin bed in their parents' home. But no, me, I'd lose mine under the stars with my favorite boy in the world on the most romantic date ever. I was ready.

Pinching his eyes closed, he rolled his forehead against mine. "No. Your first time, it should be special, it should—"

"It should be you," I cut him off. "It should be here with you. Because my first time should be exactly how I want it. And I want you." I kissed one closed eye. "Here." And the other. "Now."

Slowly his eyes slid open. He lifted his head from mine, the small wrinkle in the middle of his forehead deep with concern. "Are you sure?"

"Absolutely." I ran my hand up and down the length of him again before giving him a long squeeze. "Positively." I had my hand on him. My dress was up around my waist. What did he think was happening here?

"Jesus," he grunted. "I knew you were trying to kill

me tonight the moment I saw you in this dress."

"Not a bad way to go, though," I reasoned.

And he smiled. It made my heart flip. It made my stomach swarm with what felt like an unfathomable amount of butterflies.

He kissed the tip of my nose. I was learning that it was our thing. I liked having an our thing with Adam.

He nestled his body between my legs, with a look of purpose on his face. And he kissed me. Slowly. Sweetly. Thoughtfully. Until he was touching me. Stroking me. Small strokes. Pulling down the top of my dress, he peppered the tops of my breasts with small, delicate kisses that made my skin break out in chills. He whispered to the middle of my chest that I was beautiful.

He ran his hands across my chest and under my bra straps, pushing them aside even as he pushed my dress higher, exposing me.

He pulled a nipple into his mouth and I shuddered beneath him as his hand climbed my thigh all the way to my core.

"Oh, God," I breathed as he sucked at me and stroked me, my heart feeling light.

He kissed his way to my other breast and flicked the tip of my nipple with his tongue. It sent a beat of electricity right to my center.

"Please," I begged, feeling like it wasn't enough. Feeling like I wanted it all. Him and me together when I came this time.

"Shhh," he soothed between nips and bites that were driving me painfully wild. "I have to get you ready.

I don't want to hurt you. Ever."

One finger entered me and then another while he kissed every available surface of skin he could reach with his mouth. And by the time he leaned back and slid his wallet from his back pocket, I was a sweaty, panting, needy pile of want.

"What are you doing?" I demanded, wanting him back between my legs, this time filling me up.

He slipped a foil packet from his wallet and opened it with his teeth. "Keeping you safe," he said, sliding his hand between us.

And then his hand went back to my heat. Two fingers slid inside of me while his thumb worked my clitoris. It was too good. It felt like the best mix of pain and pleasure. He bit the skin beneath my ear and whispered there, "Come for me, Liv."

And it wasn't long before I did. Before my eyes flew open. The stars may have been swirling above me, but I was falling. So hard. So fast. And before I came down, he was there, right at my entrance, pushing in, his thumb to my nub still, his lips to mine.

One hard thrust and he was in, while I was still descending, the slight sting only heightening the drop.

He was full hilt, his breathing labored, and completely still when he kissed me hard. Kissed me like I was the only girl he'd ever kissed in his life. He kissed me like I was his first and his last. He kissed me like I was the only thing keeping him alive. He kissed me like he owned me. He kissed me like I owned him.

And when he wrenched his mouth away and laid

his cheek to mine, I expected him to pin me to the floor and have his filthy dirty way with me. I'd seen videos. I'd heard rumors. I knew how boys fucked.

But I should have known better. Because this was Adam.

"Okay?" he whispered.

A tear slid down my cheek before I even felt it hit my eye. "I'm better than okay,"

I breathed, afraid this sweet boy was about to have me a sobbing mess on one of the most important nights of my life. "I'm the best."

His cheek slid across mine until our eyes connected. His hand came to my cheek and he wiped my stray tear with his thumb before he began to move above me. In me. He set a slow pace and I watched as he went from my sweet, thoughtful Adam until he lost himself. Until he pushed into me one last time with a grunt that stole my breath all over again.

Most girls' first time would be a fumbling mess of hands and teeth and pain. But not mine. No, mine would be a night I'd think back on the rest of my life as one of the most romantic experiences ever. My boy with the tattoos had given me the stars. It made me want to give him the universe.

CHAPTER 18

Liv

"H appy Birthday!" I heard shouted from behind me. I turned around to find Braden and Mel there. Both wore smiles, so I plastered one on my face, too. I'd done a good job of avoiding the hell out of Mel lately. I was still supremely pissed about the fact she'd ratted me out to God knows who. It could have been my stepmother. It could have been Sebastian. All I knew was that Sheriff Rothchild knew exactly where to find me. Whenever I thought about sharing that with her and, her tattling on me like we were six and not sixteen, well, seventeen now, it made me want to scream.

"Thanks," I said to Mel, not really feeling thankful at all, but petty as hell instead.

Braden walked toward me and pulled me in for a hug. "Happy Birthday, gorgeous. Got any big plans?"

I did. I had the same plans I did most nights. My plans were to go home and then wait until everyone was asleep and sneak out to see my boyfriend.

Adam. Jesus. I couldn't even think of him without becoming all moony-eyed. I mean, he made me crazy before but now that we'd made love something had changed. My feelings had grown. I felt this connection to him that seemed so much deeper than before and way more grown-up. Maybe more grown-up than I was ready for because he made me want to do crazy things like forget this school, these fake people and their stupid, snobby island and run away with him.

Thank God Adam was a hell of a lot more responsible and rational than I was.

"Thanks, Braden." I pulled out of our hug and put a little distance between our bodies. I didn't want to give him the wrong impression. Because despite his flirtations and advances that door was firmly closed. Hell, it was locked. Even if Adam and I weren't a thing, Braden and I would never be. I was coming to believe he maybe was a nice guy, but he wasn't my type. He was, however, patient and always cool with me when I turned him down. He was easygoing. Way different than Sebastian in that sense. He was still a playboy, but if I never dated him I didn't anticipate any problems with the guy.

"Nope, no plans. Just a birthday dinner with Sebastian and Georgina and then bed." God, I was getting so good at lying. I didn't know whether to be proud or ashamed.

Braden pulled his bottom lip into his mouth and gave it a good suck before saying, "Or you could just go out with me. I promise I'll show you a good time."

Ha! I bet he would. That lip suck said it all.

"No, thanks. I'm tired tonight and I think I need to wash my hair." I threw back jokingly.

Slamming his hand to his chest, he clutched at his T-shirt over his heart. "Damn, Liv, you sure do know how to hurt a guy." He turned to Mel. "Did she use the old washing her hair excuse?"

Mel giggled. "She did."

"That's what I thought. I can see there's no hope here. Have a good evening, ladies." He gave us a mock salute and left Mel and I standing in the hallway alone.

I didn't know what to say. It was awkward as hell. I wasn't ready for a fight and she looked like she wanted me to say something, anything really.

I pulled my bookbag up on my shoulders higher and headed toward the front door of the school.

I hadn't made it ten feet when she said, "Why are you mad at me?"

"I'm not mad," I lied, not turning around. I kept walking and it wasn't long before I heard her footsteps right behind me.

"Yeah, you are."

I tried to ignore her and just keep on walking, but she wouldn't let up and finally she grabbed my arm and pulled me to a stop in the courtyard of the school.

"What's wrong?" she demanded like she didn't already know.

I'd finally had it with her shit and all of a sudden I was jonesing for that confrontation I'd been avoiding for days. "You told on me. I told you a secret, Mel. Something I told no one else and you told."

Her hand fell from my arm and I could see her throat working as she swallowed. She shuffled back a step and stared at the ground.

That's what I thought. She'd done it and now there was no taking it back. She couldn't even defend herself. It only pissed me off more.

I spun on my heel and started walking home. It was one of the rare days I didn't have anything after school and it was my birthday. I shouldn't have to deal with this shit.

Pounding footsteps behind me told me Mel was running toward me.

"Wait, Liv. I'm sorry. I was worried about you." She fell into step beside me, short of breath. "You can't be mad that I was worried."

I shook my head. "No, I'm mad at myself. I thought you were the one person I could trust. I was so wrong. But I won't make that same mistake again."

I kept walking even when she stopped again. "Come on, Liv. Give me a break!" she shouted from behind me but fuck her. I was done with people like that. I didn't need any more negativity in my life than I already had. And I had plenty back at the house.

But I knew in my heart it was short-lived. Less than a year and I'd be out of there and at college, and Georgina and this place wouldn't have a hold on me. And once I had the money my father left me, I wouldn't need her help anymore. I thanked God every day my father had the good sense to leave me that money and not Georgina because it was becoming all too clear the woman had probably only married him for his money. I hated that. I hated to think that my father had been duped by her. He'd loved her.

I entered the house to an excited Harry. We raced each other up the steps and I dropped my bookbag onto the floor in my room and unpacked my books and homework. I was an hour into it when Georgina texted me that dinner was ready.

I almost rolled my eyes at how impersonal that was. It was my birthday, damn it. I could smell cooked chicken as I walked down the steps and disappointment hit me hard. Dad always took me for Mexican on my birthday and Georgina knew that. We hadn't done that since he'd passed. We hadn't done a lot of anything since he'd been gone.

The table was set. The fine china was out and pale pink napkins lay next to the plates. I smiled because my dad hated those napkins. He didn't much like anything pink or floral print.

Georgina smiled behind a glass of wine at the head of the table and I sat in the seat to her right. "Happy Birthday, Princess."

Princess. She used to call me that before Dad died. Ya know, when she was still pretending she liked and cared about me. I sometimes wondered if it was all an act or if my dad's death had changed her. Either way, now, it sucked.

"Thank you."

The cook brought out a meal of baked chicken and salad and I knew there wouldn't be any cake. God, how

I missed my beloved Mexican food.

I was halfway through my piece of chicken when Sebastian finally decided to join us. My spirits wilted as he sat down. We'd almost made it through the meal without him.

"Sebastian, how nice of you to join us. No football practice today?"

Even I could see the boy was a sweaty mess. Georgina was too busy drinking her wine and living in her own little world. I almost felt bad for him in that moment and then I remembered what an ass he was to me.

"I just finished with practice." A plate of food was placed in front of him and he ate it in record time.

Shoveling the last bit of food in his mouth, he found my eyes across the table briefly before looking down again. "Happy Birthday, Livingston."

It was awkward to say the least. We didn't typically say anything nice to each other. Before my dad died we were indifferent to each other and after when he started being creepy, I avoided him like the plague. "Thanks, Seb," I muttered, placing my fork in my empty plate, wishing this meal would just be the hell over so I could hide in my room until I met Adam in the field tonight.

"So I've been thinking about the ball."

Oh hell, I didn't like it at all when Georgina got to thinking about anything. First, it was the classes, and then some crazy extravagant dress, and then Braden. No telling what she was going to come up with now.

I fidgeted with the napkin in my lap. "Yes?"

"Well, we need a theme. It's only two weeks away now. I was just going to go with pale pink. But I'm curious, if you would like a particular theme for the dance?"

It slipped out before I even knew what I was saying. "The stars."

Sebastian's head snapped up and his eyes met mine with an intensity that made my bones feel like they were shaking in my skin.

"The stars! How lovely. That's a brilliant idea. So romantic," Georgina exclaimed, taking a big sip of her wine.

Even though I was looking at anything but Sebastian, I could still feel his eyes on me. Searing me with their glare.

I gave Georgina a genuine smile. It was obvious she thought my idea was a good one and she hardly ever gave me a compliment. Despite how I loathed her sometimes, I still craved praise like any other young girl.

"The stars it is!" Georgina toasted to the air since Sebastian and I didn't have wine glasses. "It's going to be beautiful. I can't wait to see you in that dress. You're going to be so lovely."

I smiled again until I remembered she wouldn't be so happy when she found out I wasn't taking Braden. But still, I was feeling pretty good. This had been a way better birthday dinner than I'd thought it was going to be.

"May I be excused?" Sebastian asked and I felt my brow rise. The boy never asked. He always just got up and left. Everyone was playing so nice tonight. It was weird.

"Of course. I didn't have the cook make any cake or dessert." Her eyes zeroed in on my big breasts. "I figured you were watching your weight."

My body curled in on itself. I slumped over at the table, trying to hide my big breasts. She'd caught me off guard. Unaware. Buttered me up before the blow. I wanted to cry.

Sebastian's chair scraped back against the floor angrily. He threw his napkin on top of his plate and practically ran from the room.

I excused myself quietly and did the same before I freaking cried my eyes out in front of that evil bitch. I was good usually. I didn't let her affect my self-esteem or self-worth. I knew I was good. I knew I was beautiful. My daddy had made sure of that.

It was after midnight when I snuck down the steps and out of the house. It was late, and I hadn't been spending enough time with my puppers since I'd met Adam, so I grabbed his leash and my blanket and we headed out together. The weather was changing. The nights were becoming colder, so I'd pulled on a thick hoodie over my T-shirt and leggings before leaving.

I smiled as I crossed the bridge. It was far, but I could still see Adam in the distance. This. This was what I'd been looking forward to for my birthday all day. I could tell he'd seen me, too, because he'd paused and all of a sudden he was sprinting across the field and then so were Harry and I.

Harry's leash and my blue blanket dropped to the ground and I jumped into Adam's arms, my lips desperate for his. He didn't disappoint. He picked me up and I wrapped my legs around his waist. Harry jumped on the big lump that was us, excited to see Adam.

"Happy Birthday, beautiful."

I sucked in a breath, shocked. "How'd you know?"

He gave me a coy smile. "I dunno. I may have stalked your social media. By the way, your Instagram is pathetic."

I wasn't into Instagram or Facebook much. Just the bare minimum and I hardly ever uploaded. I liked to live in the moment. God only knew how many of those you had left.

I hugged him hard around the neck. "Thanks for the birthday wishes."

He pulled back and looked down at me, concern coloring his features. "Was it a good day?"

I snuggled into him again. "It is now."

Adam laid out the blanket, but I never let go. It was awkward and hilarious and really good entertainment watching him try to get that blanket down for us while I clung to him like a spider monkey.

He sat us down, me straddling his lap, my legs still wrapped around him. He leaned back on his hands. "Are you ever going to let me go?"

"Never," I whispered back. The fever was back and he wasn't even touching me. And I knew in that moment. It wasn't the fever. It was love. God, I loved this boy so much, I was burned up with it.

"I have a present for you."

I leaned back in his lap. "You do?"

He grinned at me shamelessly. And Lord have mercy, he was so delicious when he did that. So ridiculously gorgeous I wanted to jump his bones right out there in that field in the open.

He lifted me out of his lap and sat me next to him effortlessly. A cold breeze bit my ears, so I pulled my hood over my head as Adam reached into the pocket of his leather jacket and pulled out a small box.

It wasn't wrapped. It was one of the foiled gold paper boxes that jewelry came in. I may have eeked a little as I took it from his open palm. I stared down at it, feeling nervous suddenly. No one had given me a gift today. No one had given me a gift for my birthday since my dad had passed.

It felt momentous, opening that box. Normally I would have ripped the top off like a maniac. But I remembered how Adam held my hand the first time. Slowly, carefully, sweetly. So, I took my time lifting the lid and pulling back the white cotton on top.

And there nestled among the white sat a gold ring. I lifted it out of the box, holding my breath. It was a thin band that opened in the front. On one end where it opened sat a star and on the other a moon. I stared at it, thinking how perfect it was. It was like they were meeting that star and that moon, much like Adam and I had met in that field that night. Adam Nova, the star, and me his Luna, the moon. It was more than perfect. It was sweet and simple and I instantly loved it. My eyes burned with emotion as I slid it on my finger. I couldn't look at him. It embarrassed me how much I loved it. How important that scrap of gold was to me. And then he took it further and really blew me away.

"That was my mom's."

My head snapped to him. "What?" I breathed, barely able to speak. No. He shouldn't give me something so precious. I didn't deserve it. I started to take the ring off my hand, but he pressed his hand over mine, stopping me.

"No. She'd want you to have it." He lay back on the blanket and pulled me along with him, until I lay across his chest. "She would have loved you and your love of the stars."

I didn't know what to say. My heart felt like it might just burst out of my chest it felt so big. And the fever was there. So strong. So hot. I couldn't stop myself. A tear slid out of the corner of my eye and onto his T-shirt beneath my head.

"I think I love you," I whispered. That's what this feeling was, right? This heat. This all-encompassing emotion that seemed to control every decision, every thought, every *thing* in my life.

His body stiffened under mine before he brought the arm wrapped around me up to brush the hair off my face. "What did you say?"

I cleared my throat nervously, scared this might take things too far. Terrified this might make him run away from me. But I was more frightened of him never knowing. Of him never understanding how I cared for him. So, I said it again, this time with more conviction. "I think I love you, Nova." I was looking at the sky. The moon was big and round and white. A full moon. And the next words came too easily because I meant them so, so much. "I think I love you to that moon and back."

His arm curled around me tighter and then his other arm came around me, too. He clutched me so tightly to him, I could hear his heart beating quickly beneath me. His breath came faster and he squeezed tighter.

And in those seconds where he said nothing at all and just held me I was so frightened. I didn't know if I'd made the biggest mistake ever or one of the best decisions of my life.

I held on to him, hoping and praying it wasn't the last time I got to do this when he tilted his head forward until his mouth was pressed to my ear. "Just so we're clear. I don't think that I love you, Livvy. I know it. I know I love you. I knew I'd love you the first time I ever saw you beneath the stars. And I know I'll love you fifty years from now. And hell, I don't just love you to that moon and back, baby. I love you to Pluto and back even if it would take me nineteen years to get there and back."

I felt like I'd died. I felt like my heart had frozen right there in my chest. I didn't have a clue what to say. I just wanted to play those words over and over again in my mind until I had them memorized forever and ever. I wanted him to write them all down and put them in a bottle and leave them right here for me every day for always.

I was stunned, shaken to my damn core, and I hadn't a clue how to navigate such a mature and adult situation, so instead I said the first thing that popped into my mind. "Nineteen years?"

His chest shook under mine as he chuckled. "Yeah. A hell of a lot longer than it takes to get to the moon and back." He gave me a squeeze.

Oh. My. God. Swoon. I was freaking out. He loved me. A whole damn lot.

"This is the best birthday ever," I whispered to no one in particular and Adam's chest shook again.

"I guess it's going to be tough topping it for next year, huh?"

Next year. He was talking about being with me next year. And he loved me. And I loved him and for a split second under the stars everything was perfect.

I figured it was the moment to drop the ball bomb on him. I'd waited as long as I could and since it was all about the love tonight I thought he'd have a hard time saying no.

"Since you love me and I love you, it only makes sense you take me to my deb ball, then."

He snickered. "I don't think me and deb balls are a thing that go together, Livvy."

I put on my best puppy dog eyes. "But they could for me, right?"

His eyes rolled even as he smiled. "Maybe."

We lay there, us two, surrounded by the darkness, but all I felt was light. The sun eventually started to creep up into the sky and Adam insisted he'd walk me home.

He kissed me a block from the house, Harry dancing around us, and watched me walk all the way home. I only knew that because I turned around approximately five thousand times to make sure, much to Harry's dismay. And there he stood, watching me, my forgotten blue blanket tucked under his arm. I'd get it from him later, I told myself, too enamored with him to care. His eyes on me were the next best thing to his hands on me.

It was 5:30 a.m. when Harry and I finally walked up the driveway to my front door. But I paused, sure I'd heard voices, grabbing Harry by his collar. It was still mostly dark out, but I could see shadows on the front porch. I tugged Harry to the side of the house so we could hide in the darkness. Kneeling down, I prayed he kept quiet and made sure to give him lots of cuddles and whispered praise.

Meanwhile I felt like I'd stepped into another universe. I couldn't believe it. Georgina did own actual pajamas and a face underneath all of that makeup. I also couldn't believe I'd just caught her kissing Sheriff Rothchild. On our porch. At five-thirty in the morning. I kneeled there, numb. I hadn't seen her kiss anyone since my daddy. Not that it wasn't fair for her to move on. But why was she hiding it? And clearly she was. The sheriff's clothes had been rumpled. And she was wearing a silk robe over God knew what. Maybe nothing. And they weren't just kissing. They had been freaking *kissing*.

Eventually they said their goodbyes and the sheriff walked down a couple of blocks and got into an unmarked car I could only assume was his personal vehicle. I peeked around the house to see Georgina watch him drive off like a lovesick fool. After I was sure she went inside, I sat down next to a bush with Harry, feeling like my world had been rocked.

Why the hell were Sheriff Rothchild and Georgina sneaking around? Why didn't they just come out and tell everyone they were dating? I couldn't think of anyone who would actually care. Did Sebastian know about it? Did Braden? What in the hell was going on?

CHAPTER 19

Adam

"You look so handsome, my son." There were tears in Dad's eyes. I tried to ignore the faint burning in mine by checking myself out in my dresser mirror. When my dad got emotional, I got emotional. We were a sensitive bunch, us Novas.

"Thanks, Dad." I adjusted the tie at my throat nervously. Never thought I'd see the day I wore a suit. Lucky for me, Dad had a friend who let me borrow his son's. A pair of old dress shoes that only pinched my feet a little out of my dad's closet and I was golden.

I looked pretty good even. The gray three-piece suit seemed a little over the top when I first saw it, but beggars couldn't be choosers. I'd put it on hoping it wasn't too ostentatious, but it actually really suited me. And it fit me like a glove. I knew Liv would love it. I got a haircut, shaved, gelled my hair back, and even put on the cologne I knew drove her crazy.

It had only been a few weeks since our night in the planetarium, but I found that every chance I got, I liked to make her crazy for me. I think she liked it as much as I did. There weren't very many opportunities for us to be alone and I couldn't sneak her into the planetarium any time I liked. I didn't want to risk my job, but the few stolen moments we had alone, we usually spent tangled together, my hands in her soft hair, my lips fused with hers. We couldn't seem to get enough of each other and every day it seemed I loved her a little more.

She made me dream, that girl. I'd long since stopped thinking we could never work out. No matter the fact she lived on Saint Ashley's and I lived in Madison. It didn't even matter that her family didn't approve. My dreamer of a girl had me dreaming. It was the happiest I'd felt in a long time, having the ability to dream again. She'd even somehow convinced me to go to this damn cotillion with her. But who was I kidding? I'd die before I let anyone else take my girl to the dance.

I hugged Pops bye and with Raven's keys in my hands, I walked down the steps to the front of the building where I had it parked. I was nervous as hell about meeting Liv's family, so I stood outside the apartment building and smoked two cigarettes. Raven would kick my ass if I smoked in her spotless car.

The drive over was as agonizing as one might think, but when I parked in the driveway and walked up the front steps to her doorway, I felt the usual excitement I did when I knew she was going to be near.

I pressed the doorbell and already I needed another cigarette. There was no answer, so I rang it once more on restless feet.

Eventually the door opened only about two feet and there stood an older woman with blond hair, painted and dressed to perfection.

"Can I help you?" she asked in a proper Southern accent.

I smiled and pulled at the collar of my shirt nervously. *Here goes nothing.*

"I'm Adam." I pushed my hand toward the crack in the door. "I'm here for Livingston."

The door opened further and the woman I could only assume was Liv's stepmother stepped out onto the porch and closed the door quietly behind her, never taking her eyes off me.

"I'm sure there's been a mistake?" she questioned.

The back of my teeth ached from this fake ass smile I had glued to my lips, but I kept it firmly in place when I responded with, "I'm Liv's date for the debutante ball."

I understood why Liv hadn't told her I was coming just by looking at the pure outrage on her face. The form-fitting white dress she was wearing looked really ridiculous against the stark redness of her face and neck. Her eyes looked like they were going to bulge out of her head and I might have laughed if I didn't feel like I needed to impress this woman to keep seeing my girl.

The door opened suddenly behind the woman. She nearly fell backward but caught herself on the doorjamb.

Liv stepped through the doorway and past the blond woman to stand right in front of me on the porch. And God she was a sight. She had a pale pink silk dress on that made her skin look angelic. It was strapless and revealed the expanse of her shoulders and tops of her breasts. My mouth watered as I took in the tight fit of the top. The bottom flared out into a huge bell. Her cheeks were pink and her hair was up and off her shoulders in some kind of intricate twist at the back of her head. Small curls hung around her beautiful makeup free face. She looked like a damn princess.

She gave me a weary look as she turned toward her stepmother. "Georgina, I see you've met Adam."

Georgina straightened from the doorjamb and stared me down before saying, "I don't understand, Livingston. I thought you were having Braden escort you." She pulled at the pearls around her neck and I was grateful I wasn't the only one uncomfortable as hell. Shame burned through me. In that moment, I wanted more than anything for me to be good enough for Liv's family. It wasn't about social status or money. I wanted them to approve.

Liv didn't seem to be the least bit nervous when she turned to Georgina and said plain as day, "I told Braden no thank you. Adam will be my date tonight."

Pure class, Liv. She didn't lose her temper. She didn't get upset.

Georgina gasped and all of a sudden the whole Southern clutching her pearls thing wasn't just a saying for being aghast as hell. "But you can't. Braden will be here any moment."

Putting her arm through mine, Liv said, "You shouldn't have invited him to take me. It isn't very fair to him." I could see she was sad for Braden. "Let's go, Adam. I don't want to be late for my big night." She pasted a smile on her face as we walked down the sidewalk, but I could see the embarrassment in her eyes.

"Livingston Rose Montgomery, don't you dare get in that car!" Georgina yelled from the front porch. Liv stopped on the sidewalk and turned back to Georgina with a sigh that told me how tired she was of all of this and not just this moment, but of all of this woman's shit in general.

"I will not have you going to the ball with that…" She paused and stared at my neck where the tattoos peeked out from the collar of my suit. She looked at me like I was shit on her shoe. Like I was a piece of trash in her perfect fucking yard. A weed in her garden. "Hoodlum!" she finished.

Liv's chest flushed red. Her eyes glared daggers. She looked positively murderous. "Then I guess you won't have me at all."

She grabbed my hand and pulled me to the car, stomping in her heels every bit of the way. I was sure her stepmother had said something, but it was hard to hear a word over the rustling of Liv's big dress as she hustled us to the car. I pulled the door open for her. She climbed in and slammed it before I had the chance. I raced around the vehicle, anxious to get in the car before Georgina chased me down.

I got in the car and cranked her up and pulled out onto the street in record time.

The car was quiet except for Liv's angry breathing.

I could tell she wanted to scream. "I'm sorry, Adam. So sorry. I honestly didn't think she'd be so ugly."

I placed my hand on her thigh and made a right turn toward the party hall where the ball was being held. "It's okay."

She shook her head. "No, it's not okay. I should have been more upfront with her. I should have told her I was going with you."

Squeezing her knee, I murmured, "But then I wouldn't have had the pleasure of being called a hood-lum." I laughed. "What the hell year is it anyway? Hoodlum? Who the hell says that anymore?"

I could see her grin from the corner of my eye a bit before immediately sobering again. "It was mean." She said the words like they pained her. Like she couldn't bear someone being mean to me.

"Hey, look at me."

She gave me her soft brown eyes that always made me want to kiss her senseless. "I have had a lot worse said to me in my life. Okay?" However, I couldn't stop myself from asking my next question. "Now, who the hell is Braden?"

She rolled her eyes and slouched back against the seat. "Just some boy she wants me to date."

"And does he want to date you?" I'd burn this island to the ground before she hooked up with Braden.

She raised her shoulders lightly and looked away, and I watched the road. That was all the answer I need-ed, but I wouldn't ruin her big night with jealousy. We'd talk about it later. I wanted tonight to be about her. I wanted it to be special for her.

I rubbed my hand from her knee up to her thigh, the dress feeling smooth beneath my palm.

"You look beautiful." And I meant it. She looked like one of those cartoon princesses from the Disney movies but only better because she was real life.

She pursed her lips and narrowed her eyes at me. "I look like a big pink cream puff."

I chuckled under my breath because she wasn't wrong about that.

"Princess Cream Puff," I murmured, waggling my eyebrows at her. "We better hurry up and get there before I pull over just so I can eat you."

Her cheeks turned the most delicious shade of red and she giggled as we pulled into the hall and I felt lighter. Like maybe this night wasn't going to be such a shit show after all.

I couldn't have possibly been more wrong.

CHAPTER 20

Liv

I f there was a way to crawl into the floorboard of
Raven's car and hide from Adam I would have. I
was past the point of embarrassed and straight up
mortified. God, I hadn't expected that Georgina would
act that bad. It was my fault for not warning her, but
in all fairness, I'd never said I was taking Braden to the
damn dance. And after the day I'd had, I was just done.
I'd had to prepare a speech Georgina had told me about
at the very last minute and I'd spent the majority of the
day getting my hair done.

Adam came around the car and helped me out of
the seat, which was no easy task in this ridiculous dress
Georgina insisted I wear. I was still angry, upset, downright pissed off. I sure hoped I could snap out of it for
Adam's sake. Georgina would be here and so would a
heap ton of kids from school. No doubt, Braden. I felt
my stomach roll as we walked up to the building.

"Wait." Adam stopped us on the sidewalk and
pulled me to him. Two fingers stroked the bottom of

my chin as he looked into my eyes. "Tonight is going to be great."

I lifted an eyebrow at him.

"Repeat after me. Tonight is going to be great."

My other eyebrow joined in on the fun.

"I can't hear you," he said, in a sing-song voice.

"What a coincidence because I'm not saying anything."

"Come on, we got this. Adam Nova and Liv Montgomery against the world. You didn't forget, did you?" His blue eyes sparkled like twin stars.

I had. For a moment I'd let Georgina upset me and get in my head. But at Adam's words my heart leaped. He hadn't let me forget. Gone was the gloom and doom boy I'd met months ago. And in his place was a romantic. If he could believe this night was going to be awesome, then I guess I could, too.

I smiled up at him. God, he looked good enough to eat. And he wasn't even dressed up like a cream puff like me. The suit he was wearing had a beautiful fit. The tattoos that poked out here and there, only made him look even better. It didn't hurt at all that he smelled like heaven.

"God, you smell good," I said, leaning forward and taking a whiff at his neck. My nose brushed the column of his throat and he let out a growl.

"You keep doing that and we're going to have to skip this party and have one of our own."

I stepped back and looked up at him with pleading eyes. "Can we?" I wasn't joking. Not even a little bit.

He grabbed me by the hand and started pulling me toward the building. "Absolutely not. This is your special night and this is also the night I get to tell all these rich fucks that Livingston Montgomery is all mine."

I grinned at the back of his head as we entered the hall. And if Adam hadn't cheered me up the decorations would have. Twinkle lights hung through the main dance hall and the room was dimly lit. A giant ball hung from the middle of the ceiling that had stars cut out of it. The light cast stars all over the wall and floor as it spun. There were stars everywhere. At least Georgina had gotten this right and respected my wishes.

The dance floor was empty, but the room was not. People littered every side and corner of the room and it didn't go unnoticed that when we entered everyone stopped and stared. A huge part of me wanted to run for the door and back to our field. Our stars. A place where people didn't judge us.

I swallowed the huge lump in my throat while Adam squeezed my hand reassuringly before spinning me around and holding me in his arms.

"Let's dance."

The music was already playing as he twirled me around and promptly began to lead me in a waltz.

My eyes widened as he led me around the floor so easily, effortlessly. I smiled despite my nerves. "How in the hell do you always manage to surprise me?"

"Hey, you underestimate the Nova men. My father taught me to dance as soon as I could walk, Liv. How else would I romance all the ladies?" He smirked.

Now that didn't surprise me a bit. José Nova was a damn flirt.

And somehow there we were in our own little world. He'd managed to do that. I barely noticed the whispers and stares. No. Just me and Adam. Against the world.

It wasn't until a boy I didn't know asked to cut in three songs later that we finally stopped dancing. Adam was gracious and stepped aside with a smile. But he stood on the outskirts of the floor and drank punch, never taking his eyes from me as I danced with boy after boy.

When he eventually cut back in, relief flooded me. I'd talked and talked until I felt blue in the face. I leaned my head against his shoulder, breathing in his familiar smell.

"Thank you," I whispered.

His chest vibrated with a quiet laugh. "You don't have to thank me. If I had to watch you dance with one more boy tonight, I was going to lose my shit. This dance is purely for my sanity."

We danced two more songs in blessed silence before I knew I should walk around the room and socialize. And I did, with Adam's hand at the small of my back. We rotated the room and talked with friends of the family and friends from school, but I made sure to avoid the corner where Georgina and Sheriff Rothchild had set up shop.

We headed to the refreshment table for drinks

when Braden stepped in front of me, blocking my way to the punch.

"Hey, Liv." His breezy smile eased my anxiety about running into him. He didn't seem upset or put out that I'd been firm in him not escorting me tonight.

Still, I only squeaked out a small, "Hey," and tried to go around him. Awkward didn't even cover how I felt about having Adam and him breathing the same air.

He ran a hand through his hair and pushed out his hand to Adam, "I'm Braden Rothchild."

Adam's wrinkle in his forehead was out in full force at the mention of Braden's name. I expected him to lose his mind or maybe push past him and completely ignore him, but what I didn't expect was what he asked next.

"Sheriff Rothchild's son?"

Braden's hand was still hanging in the wind, so he pulled it back and stuck it in his suit pocket. "Yep, that's me."

"Hmm." Adam grunted back at Braden and awkward shot to a whole new level.

So, I intervened. My Southerness wouldn't have it any other way. "Braden, this is Adam. My escort for tonight and my boyfriend every other day."

Braden's eyes widened, but his smile never wavered. "Cool. Nice to meet you, man."

Adam didn't even attempt a "likewise" or "fuck the hell off." He just stood there, rooted to the spot, staring at Braden.

"Well, we are on our way to get some punch if you'll excuse us."

"Of course, but save a dance for me," he called out as we walked around him. I felt Adam's entire body stiffen beside me.

I grabbed his hand and steered him to the punch bowl, worried out of my mind there was about to be a brawl at my ball. Although it did have a certain ring to it. Brawl at the ball.

I poured a glass of punch while Adam leaned against the refreshment table stewing. So much for this is gonna be an awesome night.

"I don't like that kid."

"What kid?"

He glared at me.

"Okay, so why don't you like Braden?" I took a sip of punch.

He crossed his arms. "There are a myriad of reasons I don't like him, the first being that he wants my girl."

I smiled. I couldn't help it. I shouldn't have. But hearing him call me his girl and get all territorial, well, it would appeal to any seventeen-year-old girl's senses.

"Come on, caveman. Let's dance," I muttered, placing my drink down.

"I'm serious, Liv."

I nodded. "I know."

He wrapped his arms around me and we swayed back and forth on the dance floor. "I don't trust him."

I paused, shocked. "What? Braden's harmless, Adam."

He leaned over and kissed the tip of my nose

and pulled me closer. "Just don't be alone with him. Promise me?"

I'd do anything for him. Especially if it was so important to him, even if I didn't understand. "Okay," I whispered.

He mumbled a quiet, "Thank you."

And we danced and I made a speech thanking Georgina for all her hard work and for everyone coming out. I made sure it was saccharine sweet just for her. We made the rounds again, this time saying hello to Mel and Sebastian. Adam was less than impressed with him as well, but he didn't let it put a damper on our night.

It was my coming out party, but I felt like it was more our coming out. Now everyone knew. And they couldn't do shit about it while we were here and dancing. No, none of these people would dare make a scene and embarrass themselves or their family's namesake.

And as the night came to a close, I made sure to say goodbye and to thank everyone for coming as they left. I couldn't have Georgina mad about that, too. I knew she was already fuming about my date for the night, if the glares from across the room were any indication.

When everyone was gone and all that was left was just the staff and me and Adam, he pulled me back to the dance floor and twirled me around until my big, pink cream puff bell of a dress floated into the air. I laughed as he snapped me back to him and dipped me low.

His lips met mine softly before he pulled me back up. "I finally have you all to myself."

"Greedy," I muttered, this time kissing him.

"Only for you."

And we danced for another hour more under the twinkling lights of at least a thousand fabricated stars.

It wasn't an awesome night. It didn't even rate in my top five nights with Adam, but it wasn't nearly as bad as I anticipated it would be.

I breathed a sigh of relief as he spun me around the floor a final time. I'd made it through the hard part. I'd let them all know they couldn't keep us apart.

Together, we were unstoppable.

Just a mere hour later, and I'd realize how wrong I could be.

CHAPTER 21

Adam

The porch light was on outside Liv's home when we pulled up. I was worried about what kind of punishment her stepmother would dole out once she went inside the house.

"Looks like she's waiting up on you," I said from my spot in the driver's seat, feeling nervous as hell.

She looked at the house anxiously, too. "Well, you better give me a kiss for good luck. I think I'm gonna need it."

I leaned over the console between us and kissed her tiny button nose.

She grabbed my tie before I could pull back. "Uh uh uh. I'm gonna need you to really lay one on me before I go to battle."

And so I did. I dipped my tongue inside her mouth, tasting the innate sweetness that was Liv, my Livvy, my Luna. I pressed my chest to hers until she was pushed all the way back against her seat and kissed the hell out of her.

And this time when I pulled back, she wrapped her hands around the back of my neck and used her thumbs to rub my cheekbones. "I love you to the moon and back, Nova." The sincerity in her eyes blew me away and I felt like the luckiest guy in the entire world.

"I love you to Pluto and back, Montgomery," I said, once again pressing my lips to hers.

Later, I'd take solace in the fact the last things we'd said to each other were the most important things either of us could have ever spoken.

Because like a bad dream, the door was wrenched open from behind me and I was on the ground. I barely had time to register the fact that two male bodies pressed me to the asphalt. One with an elbow to the throat and the other with a knee to the stomach. A barrage of limbs and hands and body parts bombarded me, disorienting me.

A scream. Liv's, I thought to myself, as I tried to fight my way off the ground, but it was a fruitless attempt. There were two of them and only me. They'd caught me off guard. It wasn't long before I was dragged across the pavement and into the driveway.

Two big guys held me up and kept my arms pinned behind me. Two more surrounded me. Braden and Sebastian. Jesus, what the hell was going on? But I couldn't focus on them. No, I could only hear Liv shouting in the distance.

Out of the corner of my eye, I saw Georgina step off the porch. She'd changed from her fancy dress and had a brown suitcase in her hand. "Get in the car, Liv."

"No!" I heard her shout. She was across the yard from me, but goons surrounding me made it hard to see her.

"You did this to yourself. Now get in the fucking car!" Georgina screamed.

I tried to fight off the two men holding me down. I pulled and I tried my hardest to rip myself free.

"Hold him down, boys," Sebastian ordered, and I felt my blood boil.

"Liv!" I screamed. "Liv!"

"Please!" I heard her cry as another man shoved her into the back of a black town car. I was going to be sick. This couldn't be happening.

Georgina threw the suitcase in the back of the vehicle before turning to look at me. In the same way she had before the dance. The way that made me feel less than. "Take out the trash, boys," she said before climbing into the driver's seat of the black town car.

She pulled onto the road as the first fist connected to my cheekbone. A blast of pain shot across my face like a bullet hitting its target, but I never took my eyes off that car. Liv's hand was against the back window, her tear-stained, hysterical face behind it.

No blow to the face could compare to seeing her like that, driving away from me.

The next blow was to my stomach and it sent me to the ground. The men holding me up let me fall to the asphalt. I lost sight of Liv and the car as I took a kick to the mouth. Blood coated my teeth and gums, the taste of metal thick on my tongue. I tried to get up. I had to get to Raven's car and then Liv.

"Stay down," Sebastian said, with a deathly calm to his voice and then I was knocked in the head from behind. Blows came from every which way. Pain radiated throughout my entire skull. My ribs screamed in agony and still I got up. Fight, my addled brain screamed at me. Fight for her. I wouldn't let her down.

It was the sickening kick to my forehead that did me in. Blood poured into my eyes. Suffering filled every inch of my body. They were going to kill me, right here in Liv's front yard with the beautiful ocean right across the fucking street. I wondered if they'd dump my body in the sea.

Through the haze of blood and pain, I saw the flashing of blue lights. The police. Thank God. Relief swept through me like a rushing current.

Everyone backed away, but try as I might, I couldn't move. I rolled on the ground, fighting the blackness that threatened to pull me under. I couldn't go there. I willed my mind to stay alert. I had to get to Liv.

The scuff of shoes on pavement made my closed eyes fly open. Not a foot from my face stood a pair of black boots that fed into a police uniform. My brief stint of relief vanished into thin air right along with the girl I loved. I was done. Fucked. Royally screwed.

"Damn, you boys did a number on him," Sheriff Rothchild said and I closed my eyes. This was it. I didn't know what would come next, but I knew it was nothing good. Not with this man involved.

A criminal.

A rapist.

He picked me up off the ground and I would've screamed and fought him if I could have, but they'd beaten the fight right out of me. I had nothing left. I was dangerously close to losing consciousness.

"Help me get him in the car, Braden."

They pushed me into the car, but not before I spat a mouthful of blood into Sheriff Rothchild's face.

He pulled a handkerchief from his pocket and wiped the blood from his cheek as he stared down at me lying across the back seat of his cruiser. "Boys, break the window in the front from the outside. Make sure it looks like a break-in. We'll call this self-defense." He didn't take his eyes off me the entire time.

He slammed the door and climbed into the front of the police car and started it up. I had no idea where he was taking me. I could barely lift my head, make a cognizant thought.

"I see why Livingston likes you so much, Adam. You got your momma's good looks for sure. Those eyes. They did me in, too."

Nausea rolled through me and I gagged as I prayed for darkness. Fuck, I wanted it to take me. I couldn't listen to him talk about my momma.

"But I warned you. I told you last time I saw you to stay away from her. But you boys from the mainland. You're dumb as shit and never fucking listen." He took a long breath. "Like that fuck-up Boone. He was supposed to be watching you and your father, but he just had to fuck with Livingston. You guys can't keep your poor dicks in your pants, can you?" He chuckled wickedly.

"I get it. I've always wanted what's not mine, too."

Tears slipped down my cheeks and onto the leather beneath me. I wanted to die. This man. He'd taken everything I loved from me. Twice now.

It wasn't long before the car came to a stop, but I couldn't even lift my head to see where we were.

He dragged me out the back of the car. "Come on, you sorry sack of shit. Stand up."

I leaned against him and he leaned down into my ear. "You won't contact Liv again, now will you? It'd be a shame if your poor father was jumped again, wouldn't it? He might not make it this time."

I sucked in a breath, shock sending a whole new wave of pain through my body. No. Not my pops.

He laughed, pure evil echoing in my ears. "What now? You didn't think that was random, did you?"

I bucked back with all my might and I spat again, this time hitting his shoe.

"You little fucker, you better be careful who you fuck with."

He dragged me across the parking lot and into a building I'd never seen the inside of in all my time in North Madison.

Two feet into the Madison County Jail, he leaned close enough so only I could hear. "Your momma. She was one of a kind. I loved it when she begged. Both times."

I squeezed my eyes closed and held my breath,

praying for blackness, but all too aware of what he was saying. "Especially the night I came to your apartment. She was creating too much of a stink. She was causing problems for me." His fetid breath made my busted lip curl. "She begged for her life. And for you as I shoved the pills down her throat, a gun to her head."

I shook my head, my brain feeling like it was swimming. "Noooo!" I screamed. Agony and misery ripping at me. I'd been too happy the past few months. It was time to pay up.

He shoved me to the floor without a care in the world. "Book him. Breaking and entering over at the Montgomery house. Aggravated assault as well. Mrs. Montgomery will be here in the morning to file a report."

I lay there bleeding and not just for myself. But for my mother. My father. For Liv.

"Don't worry, Adam. Braden will take care of Liv," Sheriff Rothchild threw over his shoulder as he left.

No. Please, no. Misery screamed in my veins. Torment blasted through me. Every bone in my body pounded. But it wasn't just pain that blazed through me as I lay on the dirty county jail floor. No, it was something far greater.

Vengeance.

To be continued...

Liv and Adam's story continues in book 2:

IN HER SPACE

November 15, 2018.

IN HER SPACE

I was reunited with Livingston Montgomery in the
broad sunshine of a Carolina morning, right where she
belonged; in the light.
It'd been too long since I'd seen her face.
She had changed, but so had I.
I was Adam Nova, reformed bad boy. Now, successful
business man.
I had it all, except for the one person I'd always wanted,
and now I was back to claim her.
She was living in the shadows, just a shell of the former
girl I knew.
But it didn't matter that she tried to hide from me in
the dark.
I'd follow her into the deepest depths of hell.
I just wanted to be In Her Space.

OTHER BOOKS BY
Amie Knight

See Through Heart

A Steel Heart

An Imperfect Heart

The Line

ABOUT THE AUTHOR

Amie Knight has been a reader for as long as she could remember and a romance lover since she could get her hands on her momma's books. A dedicated wife and mother with a love of music and makeup, she won't ever be seen leaving the house without her eyebrows and eyelashes done just right. When she isn't reading and writing, you can catch her jamming out in the car with her two kids to '90s R&B, country, and showtunes. Amie draws inspiration from her childhood in Columbia, South Carolina, and can't imagine living anywhere other than the South.

FACEBOOK: www.facebook.com/authoramieknight

TWITTER: www.twitter.com/AuthorAmieKnigh

GOODREADS: www.goodreads.com/AmieKnight

INSTAGRAM: www.instagram.com/amie_knight

WEBSITE: www.authoramieknight.com

GROUP: www.facebook.com/groups/amieknightssocialites

NEWSLETTER: http://eepurl.com/cPHIuT

Made in the USA
Columbia, SC
26 May 2020